AMETHYST EYES
The Legend Comes to Life

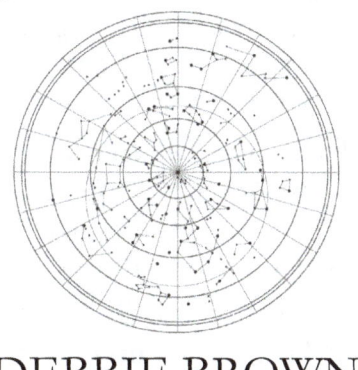

DEBBIE BROWN

AMETHYST EYES: THE LEGEND COMES TO LIFE
By
Debbie Brown
Copyright © Debbie Brown 2014
Cover Illustration Copyright © 2014 by Ravenswood Publishing
Published by Mythos Press
(An Imprint of Ravenswood Publishing)

GMTA Publishing Group
6296 Philippi Church Rd.
Raeford, NC 28376
http://www.gmtapublishing.com

Printed in the U.S.A.

ISBN-13: 978-0692304556
ISBN-10: 069230455X

Dedication

I want to dedicate this book to my girls, Zoey and Savannah. Your arrival, Savannah, pushed the release of this book back by a year, testing my ability to focus, and giving the story time to mature. I love you both. Thank you, Chris, for your patience and feedback, I do appreciate it all. Kim, and Ursula, as always, your comments mean a lot to me. A special thanks to Kelly, for your critical eye and honest opinion.

Finally, I want to say thank you, Kitty, my amazing publisher, for your belief in my work, for your hard work and relentless efforts to get all of your authors out there. HUGS! We are lucky to have you.

TABLE OF CONTENTS

Chapter 1

A burst of adrenaline shot through Tommy's veins as he caught sight of the small shuttle through the domed ceiling. He took a shaky breath, filling his lungs with the earthy smells of the arboretum, and closed his eyes. With all his attention focused on the link, he reached out to make contact with his father. He wanted, no, *needed* to know if his father was on that ship, but he got nothing…yet again. Lifting his eyes to the moving indigo lights, he stood with the intention of heading down to the docking bay. He hoped to find his father there, or at least get some answers.

A twig snapped behind him. He shifted to see Jayden slipping into his private corner of the arboretum. Of course, she'd have known where to find him. Unlike the rest of the people on board, Tommy didn't have the interface chip imbedded in his neck that linked him to the main computer. He wore a temporary one he could remove at will, which is what he'd done before coming out here to mull over his thoughts.

He frowned, taking in her grey, two-tone medical uniform that indicated her transition from student to cadet. "Why are you wearing that?" She had not bothered to tell him what rotation she would be starting tomorrow, and now he knew why. He smiled to himself as he tried to imagine Jayden working alongside the chief medical officer, her father.

Ignoring the question, she dropped down on the old wooden bench and lifted her gaze upward to search the stars. Tommy shook his head and settled down beside her. "There," he said, pointing to the shuttle. They'll reach us soon enough". He caught the flicker of relief that crossed her features. "Any news from your father?" he asked, secretly hoping to know if she had any news about his own father, the ship's commander.

She shook her head and brought her attention to the weathered planks of the bench. "It looks like the one Two-Feathers has at the farm house." Placing her palm flat against the wood, she slid her fingers along the worn grain.

Tommy nodded. It had been his mother's favorite bench, but he had never shared that bit of information with Jayden. Nor had he ever told her about all the memories it held, and at the moment, he wasn't up to it. He was worried about his father, and about the fact that he had not felt any contact through their link for days now. He knew his father had felt his mother's death through the link, even though he'd been far from Earth at the time, and since Tommy had had no such feeling, he held on to the belief that his father was still alive.

"I can't believe you've already been here three years," she said, cutting into his thoughts.

Tilting his head in her direction, he studied her a moment and chuckled under his breath. "Didn't think I'd last this long, did you?" Her green eyes locked with his, and he found himself admiring how their gold flecks lit up.

She snorted. "Nope, not even a week."

He nodded. "That's about how long you'd known me before you accidentally poisoned me, wasn't it?"

Her face turned bright red and she looked away. "It was an accident. I didn't know you were allergic to banja jelly." She kept her focus on the ground.

With all his attention on her, he paused as her attire registered again. "Why exactly are you wearing that?"

She shrugged with one shoulder as she smoothed the sleeve of her uniform down with her hand. "I was going to go to medical bay and get a feel for it before the start of rotation." Squaring her shoulders, she brought her gaze back to him. "Before father got back."

Tommy grinned, thinking about how volatile she could be. In all honesty, he had a hard time imagining her in the role of a reassuring care-giver, but he'd been wrong before. "And here I thought you wanted to work on your delightful bedside manner," he teased.

She swatted him none too gently on the arm. "Better hope I'm not on duty when you come crawling in, needing assistance." Her fire was back.

He winced and rubbed his shoulder in mock pain. "And give you the chance to finish me off? Trust me, I know better than that." He pulled away and increased his pace to get away from her, but not fast enough to avoid the blow to the back of his knees that sent him sprawling into the dirt. He coughed, swiftly rolled over, and scrambled to pin her beneath him, a smile curling at the corner of his mouth.

Locking her smaller wrists in his hand, he stood and effortlessly lifted her to her feet, not bothering to dust himself off. Standing almost a foot taller, he easily guided her towards the door with one hand on her shoulder, all while keeping a firm grip on her wrists. He wasn't going to let her try that twice.

"What's going on here?" A grating voice startled Tommy and he relinquished his hold on Jayden.

The teens turned slowly towards the voice, and Tommy's stomach knotted as he came face to face with Fardoc's sour expression. Ever since the botanist had arrived on board, a little over two weeks ago, he'd delighted in making Tommy's life miserable. At least that's how it seemed to Tommy. The arboretum had always been the one place on the ship Tommy was able to find a semblance of Earth, and this man seemed determined to keep him out of it.

"Nothing, Chief Fardoc," Jayden answered. "I fell and Tommy was just helping me up." She shifted uneasily, betraying her apprehension. Tommy had to give her credit for being gutsy enough to hold the chief's glare. Jayden didn't like the botanist either, and less so since he'd started undoing what Jayden's mother had created in the arboretum. Tommy knew this because of the fit she threw two nights ago

"If you had been walking, instead of running, then you might not have fallen." He stared her down with his coal black eyes. Curling his lip in disgust he added, "You can be sure I will inform the commander of your intrusions."

"Please, enlighten me," the Commander said as he appeared alongside the group. He stood tall, his amethyst eyes stern as he took in the situation.

Fardoc whirled away from the teens, unable to hide his frustration. With a slight tilt to his head, he brushed his unkempt black hair from his eyes and launched into his explanation. "Sir, these cadets have been a constant disruption to the arboretum. I have attempted to settle into my duties as chief botanist, while assuming the overwhelming task of bringing the arboretum back up to expected standards." He waved an arm in Tommy and Jayden's direction. "And having them run wild throughout the area-"

"The arboretum is already above established standards!" Jayden spat out in anger. "My mother had made sure of that." She crossed her arms and challenged Fardoc with her stance.

"Thank you, Jayden, but if you will allow me to handle this…" the commander said, a hint of warning in his voice. He turned back to the flustered botanist. "This cadet is correct in stating that the outdated standards had been abandoned some time ago. You would do well to inform yourself of the standards upheld on the Phoenix –before you make any changes." He held the crewman's gaze. "You will also take note that the arboretum is open to any and all crewmembers, including their families, at all times, day or night."

Tommy watched as Fardoc's pale face turned bright red, a strange contrast against his green and gold jumpsuit. He wondered how long this guy would last if he openly defied the commander.

"How am I supposed to maintain a healthy growth environment in the arboretum if there is no control over what goes on in here?" He clenched his fists but left his arms at his sides.

"Come now, Chief. In nature, there is no such thing as a controlled environment. This is a sanctuary for the crew members as well as a nursery for the plants we use in colonisations. I suggest you run any proposed changes by me prior to implementation." The commander's tone left no room for negotiation. "Dismissed."

Eyes wide, Fardoc's mouth dropped open for a second before he clamped it shut. "Yes, Commander," he said through clenched teeth. He spun on his heel and stiffly walked away without another word.

Tommy sensed that his father was tired and in no mood for any of this. He prayed that Jayden would hold her tongue, then cringed inwardly when he heard her draw in a breath, a sure sign she was about to launch into a rant. The commander silenced her with a sharp glare and Tommy quickly turned away from Jayden to hide his reaction.

With a nod of his head, the commander ushered them out of the arboretum and away from the lush, earthy smells. Jayden paused as they stepped into the ice-blue corridor. "Has my father returned as well, Commander?"

He gave a curt nod. "He accompanied an injured crewmember

to medical bay," he said tensely.

That didn't help his father's mood, Tommy thought.

"Well then if you'll excuse me, Commander, Tommy," Jayden said quickly, "I shall join him."

Tommy gave her a slight nod before she scurried off, but she ignored him. "Have you eaten, Father?" He turned to his father, relieved to have him back. They weren't often apart for more than a day or two at a time, but this mission had kept his father away for the past twelve days.

Looking up, the commander met his son's eyes. The familiar, silent exchange passed from one set of amethyst eyes to the other. "No, not since yesterday," he confessed.

This admission startled Tommy. What had he been doing that he couldn't find time to eat? "I thought you'd want to eat in the dining hall, but if you prefer not to, we could eat in our quarters." Tommy loved the food in the dining hall, but still didn't feel comfortable going alone. The overly formal atmosphere was more enjoyable with others, even though conversation around the table was not permitted.

Amusement lit the commander's eyes. "I assure you, I would be civil enough to eat in public. However, I had hoped to discuss some things with you over end-of-day meal." He paused at a junction in the corridor. "I have to meet with the doctor a moment regarding Watoo's condition before we eat."

Tommy's stomach lurched. No! Not Watoo! "Could I go with you, Father?" Although Watoo had been Tommy's teacher when he'd first come on board, they'd since become good friends. Tommy's stomach knotted.

The commander clenched his jaw momentarily and tugged on his black and blue uniform top. "Could I ask that you set out our meal and I will inform you of the doctor's prognosis? I shall not be gone long." He placed a hand on Tommy's shoulder and made contact through the link. "I would not want you to see Watoo in his present condition." His expression softened a little. "Not yet."

Reluctantly, Tommy agreed. He had never been in the habit of going against his father's requests, but then he wondered if Jayden was going to get to see Watoo…

Making his way along the corridor to his quarters, he wrestled with his emotions regarding his friend. Tommy had not been given the chance to say goodbye to his mother. The last moments of consciousness following the accident were focused on joining the pendant, on contacting his father, while his mother slipped away. He swallowed back the memory. What if Watoo didn't make it either?

Tommy paused by a large porthole and stared out at the slow-moving stars. Slamming his hand against the edge of the window, he made his decision. His father would have to accept it. Drawing in a breath, he squared his shoulders and headed for medical bay.

The commander was waiting for Tommy by the entrance as the doors parted, causing him to jump back with a start. Feeling his face flush, Tommy realized his father must have been privy to all of his thoughts as he'd broadcast them through their link. A wave of calm energy flowed from his father, surrounding Tommy, easing his nerves. The commander nodded for his son to follow.

"Commander." The doctor stepped through the particle curtain and became visible. His weary voice matched his harried appearance. Tommy noted that Watoo was not in the common bed pod area, but that he had been isolated to the critical care section.

This can't be good, Tommy thought. He reached up absently to activate the chip in his uniform collar, which would allow him to see through the particle curtain. He frowned when Watoo's bed remained concealed.

The doctor gave a half nod of acknowledgement in Tommy's direction before he launched into a status report. "He's been placed in a regenerative field, and we've done the preliminary work installing blood cell generators along the humerus and ulna."

Tommy grabbed the doctor's arm. "Wait, aren't they supposed to be placed along the femur for maximum output?" He looked from his father to the doctor and his mouth went dry. "Why aren't they in his legs? And why can't I see through the particle curtain?" His heart hammered in his chest while his mind raced through possible scenarios.

"Doctor," a voice came from the other side of the curtain.

Tommy's father followed the doctor through, but Tommy wasn't sure if he could go, so he held back. A twinge in the pit of his stomach caught his attention, and he turned instinctively. His gaze settled on Jayden, hunched over in a chair at the far end of the room. He frowned, looking her over carefully before he silently moved towards her. Laying a hand on her shoulder, he dropped down on one knee at her side.

Puffy eyes and a blotchy face were revealed as she raised her head. A strangled sound escaped her lips and she leaned into his embrace, trembling.

The image of Watoo's injured form flashed in Tommy's mind, unsettling him. Watoo's lower body had been crushed and mangled beyond recognition. It would take a miracle for him to survive injuries this severe, Tommy acknowledged grimly. He'd spent enough time helping out in medical bay to know that he would not be able to see Watoo for some time. The medical team had enough to do if they were to save his friend. "Come on," Tommy said as he lifted Jayden to her feet. "Let's get out of here." In silence, he escorted her through the door and along the corridor towards their quarters. Stepping off the lift, he guided her to her door, but she shook her head.

"I don't want to be alone." She choked back a sob.

He nodded. "OK, I don't think my father will mind, at least until he comes home to eat." His insides shook as he walked three doors down to the quarters he shared with his father. He couldn't get the image of his friend out of his mind…even if he didn't know where it had come from.

Jayden let herself be guided to the sitting area where Tommy eased her onto the sofa. He stood over her, not knowing what to do. "Want something to drink?"

Keeping her attention on the floor, she shrugged. He lightly touched her shoulder before going to the replicator for some apple juice. Moving about on autopilot, he wondered what had happened to injure his friend so badly.

He settled himself onto a seat across from Jayden and tried to swallow a sip of his juice, but the strange twinge in his stomach made it difficult. He assumed it was from the image in his mind and took a few breaths to try and calm himself. Jayden stared blankly across the floor, cup in hand. "Did you see him?" he asked cautiously, not wanting to provoke an outburst.

Her shoulders shook and she drew in a breath with an audible shudder. Raising her head to face him, he saw tears glisten in the corners of her eyes before they slipped silently down her cheeks. Biting her lower lip, she twisted her mouth. "The aide tried to stop me from crossing the particle curtain, but I wanted to see Father, so I shoved past." She swiped at her tears with the back of her hand. "I mean, I'm starting my medical rotation tomorrow, so I'm allowed in with patients now…"

Tommy rose and moved around the table to sit at her side. Offering a soft cloth to wipe her eyes, he let her lean into him and held her as she cried. They sat there quietly for a while, the silence broken only by the occasional tortured sounds she made.

The door opened, admitting the commander and the doctor. Jayden stiffened. Reluctantly, Tommy let go of her and stood, offering her a hand as she tried to rise. He turned toward his father, afraid of what he had to say.

The doctor moved to Jayden's side without a word and guided

her back towards the door. "Wait," Tommy called out. "Aren't you going to tell us how he's doing?" He flinched when his father laid a hand on his shoulder, but he didn't miss the exchange between the two men. "Father, please, tell us how he is."

Letting out his breath, the commander shot a glance in the chief medical officer's direction and gestured for Tommy to sit. Mathezar nodded, said something only Jayden could hear, and moved her back towards the sofa. "Watoo is still alive," the doctor said. His tone was far from reassuring, his expression grim.

Tommy, still standing, turned his attention to the doctor. "But you're not sure he'll live." his voice sounded hollow.

"No." The doctor passed a hand through his dark hair and settled down onto the couch beside Jayden. Without looking up he added, "I don't understand how he is even alive at this point."

"Does he have a chance?" Tommy asked, needing reassurance.

"Thomas," his father spoke softly, moving closer to his son. "I know he was a good friend of yours—"

Tommy spun to face his father, feeling tears well in his eyes. "*Is*, is a good friend, and I have to see him…to say goodbye." His voice cracked. The link swelled, offering support and comfort.

"Mathezar?" the commander asked. "The decision is yours."

The doctor rubbed a hand over his tired eyes as he let out a breath. "I would prefer if we gave him some time to rest rather than disturb him, but I promise to alert you immediately if his condition worsens " He spoke softly to Jayden and they both stood. "I'll see you in an hour or so."

Nervously walking around the room, Tommy barely acknowledged the doctor as he left with his daughter. He didn't know how to handle the situation. He didn't want to have to deal with it. As far as he was concerned, he'd already lost enough. He wondered if Two-Feathers could be of any help. The old shaman had proven his abilities in the past, but as reason kicked in and Tommy remembered the image of his injured friend, he knew nothing short of a miracle would save Watoo now.

"Thomas," his father's voice broke the silence. "We should eat, and I still have things I need to discuss with you."

Tommy looked up and composed himself as best he could. Nodding, he headed toward the dining area. "I don't have much of an appetite left, Father," he admitted. He studied his father. It wasn't often his father looked this tired. "What happened to all of you?"

With a wave of his hand, the commander motioned for Tommy to sit as the door chime sounded. Stepping aside to allow the two crewmembers to deliver the platters of food, Tommy was surprised to see the two-piece black uniforms from the dining hall. They didn't normally deliver the food themselves. "Thank you," Tommy said as the crewman removed the domed cover, allowing the enticing aroma to greet him and stir his appetite. OK, maybe he was a little hungry.

The commander sat next to his son and waited for the door to slide shut behind the crewmembers. Closing his eyes, he drew in a long, steadying breath.

Tommy studied his father, his concern growing. When he tried to reach out to his father through the link, a wave of panic plowed through as he realized that the access had been closed off. Attempting to surround him with his own energy, Tommy opened his side of the link as an offering, almost like an energy charged hug.

The corner of his father's mouth lifted into a tired smile. "Thank you."

Swallowing the dry lump that had formed in his throat, Tommy held his father's gaze. "What's wrong?" He straightened his shoulders, not looking away. "Why won't you let me in?" Tommy suppressed a shudder. He was beginning to fear the worst.

The commander lifted a glass of farou tonic. Currants of orange and yellow liquid swirled about as he drank, instantly perking him up. Tommy remembered the effect the drink had had on him when he himself had consumed it. "Eat," his father ordered.

Lifting the fork to his mouth without paying attention to its contents, Tommy openly watched his father, trying to sense something through the link, trying to understand what had happened on the planet. "I thought this was to be a simple colony transfer," Tommy said, his tone casual.

The commander exhaled sharply. "It should have been." He took another sip of his tonic, ignoring the food on his plate. At least the plates kept the food warm, and if he did decide to eat, the temperature would be just right.

Tommy rammed his hand through his hair out of frustration and tossed his fork down onto the table, immediately getting his father's attention. "Tell me." He placed a hand on his father's forearm and caught his tired gaze. The flash was brief, but came with an intensity that surprised Tommy. He wasn't able to make out any clear images through the chaos, but the emotions were strong and reeked of fear. "You were attacked." It wasn't a question.

"Ambushed, would be more accurate." He turned away from Tommy's scrutiny and stood, almost as though he wanted to put some distance between them.

Tommy pressed his lips together. "Why won't you tell me? I'm eighteen now." He played his card, hoping to force the issue, since he was finally no longer considered a child in this society.

The commander turned slowly to face Tommy, his jaw clenched. He let out a sharp breath. "Very well..." Motioning for his son to join him in the sitting area, he gasped, his step faltering as he clutched at his side.

Tommy flew over the sofa and grabbed hold of his father who stumbled and sank to the floor. A spatter of blood trickled from his mouth and Tommy watched in horror as his father's eyes rolled back and closed before his breathing went still. "Medical emergency!" Tommy shouted to the CPU, the omnipresent computer. The life-force alarm sounded and the doctor tore into the room seconds later, Jayden on his heels.

Tommy laid his father gently on the floor and moved back to let the doctor work. Dr. Tounga joined Mathezar and immediately placed a cardio-respiratory stimulator on his father's chest. "He's still not breathing," Tommy whispered.

Tounga handed the chief medical officer an object Tommy had never seen, even after having helped out in medical bay these past three years. The small, dimly lit cube didn't seem to have any controls whatsoever, but as soon as the doctor placed it near the commander's neck two thin wires appeared. "Hold his shoulders," the doctor told Tommy.

Hands firmly on his father's shoulders, Tommy kept his gaze riveted to the mysterious cube. The thin wires probed the neck area, and the cube began to glow as they slipped beneath the skin, honing in on their target. "Oh my God! Is that thing alive?" Tommy shuddered as he watched the cube imbed itself into his father's neck until only a slightly raised, brightly glowing layer remained. His father's color immediately pinked.

The commander began to twist, obviously in pain. Tounga and Tommy held him firmly while the doctor adjusted the instrument on the commander's chest. As soon as the commander relaxed, Tounga did too. Tommy didn't miss the odd look Tounga shot his senior officer.

The doctor sat back on his heels and let out a breath of relief. "It doesn't work for everyone, but the Sulaurian jellyfish feeds off the blood's toxins and gases while re-oxygenating the blood. It also supports the kidneys." He added absently.

Tommy watched the doctor wave two medical aids over. Silently, efficiently, they lifted his father onto a M.A.G. (magnetic anti-gravity) stretcher and rushed off to medical bay. Tommy was barely two steps behind and obviously so was Jayden, who grabbed hold of his arm when he tried to follow the group behind the particle curtain. She placed a hand firmly on his chest. "Let them work," she said to Tommy, still holding his arm.

He turned his head hesitantly away from the particle curtain to search her eyes. Warmth spread across his chest from where she'd placed her hand.

She shook her head, holding him firmly in place. "You know my father will call you the instant he knows something."

"I just can't leave him." Tommy made a face as Jayden attempted to pull him towards the door.

"Look, let's just take a walk around the ship's perimeter to give them a few minutes to get him settled." She pulled at his arm again. "Come on, just a few minutes. We'll be right outside." Her eyes softened and she nodded towards the door once more.

Letting out a breath of frustration, Tommy let himself be dragged out of medical bay. He knew she was right, but he was afraid to leave his father's side, afraid to lose another parent and afraid to really be alone in the universe. Watoo's accident had shaken Tommy a little too much.

"Are you even listening to me?" Jayden asked, sounding only slightly annoyed.

Tommy blinked and looked around the corridor. He shook his head. Had she really been talking? The view out the port window caught his eye. "Where's the pod?" He whirled around to face her.

"What the heck happened to them?" He caught a fleeting look cross her face as she shrugged and turned and stepped away.

"Father didn't tell me." She kept walking.

Leaning into the port window he strained for a better view. The disk-shaped transfer pod was nowhere to be seen. He hurried past Jayden, a third of the way along the corridor and looked out the porthole. The arboretum was there, affixed to the underside of the main disk. Increasing his speed he made his way another third around the circular corridor. This pod was missing as well. They must have sent it to pick up the first one.

"Why are you running?" Jayden asked as she caught up to him.

He reached out and grasped her by the shoulders. Maybe her father didn't tell her anything, but she must have heard something by now. "Spill." His tone was a little rougher than he'd intended.

She grimaced under his grasp. "I don't know any-"

"Don't lie to me." Anger rose from deep inside. He was about to ask her again when a flash caught him off guard. Something had bitten his father during the attack on his crew. Releasing a shocked Jayden, he left her standing in the corridor and raced back to medical bay.

Tommy barely missed colliding with a medical aide as he ran through the doors. A quick glance to his left told him the doctor wasn't in his office. Activating the chip in his collar, he scanned the room. They probably hadn't thought of changing the modulation. He was wrong.

"Can I help you?" Petra blocked Tommy's path. She brushed

her white hair from her forehead, while her bright green eyes locked onto his.

Tommy couldn't help it, he bit back a smile. She reminded him of a pixie, and in her braced stance, she came across as an angry Tinkerbell. "I need to see Mathezar, please," his voice sounded as worried as he felt. "It's important."

She raised a delicate hand to his cheek. "Wait here; I'll see what I can do." She turned with a slight bounce and headed behind the particle curtain.

Mathezar stepped out from behind the curtain and motioned Tommy closer. He looked as harried as he had when he'd first returned to the ship with Watoo. Could that have been only a few hours ago?

"Did you find anything?" Tommy asked. His insides shook as his concern for his father grew.

Passing a hand over his tired eyes the doctor shook his head. "We've stabilized him, but have yet to identify the cause."

"Did you find any bite marks on him?"

"What?" The doctor seemed to perk up. "What do you know?"

"Look, just call it a hunch, but what if he had been bitten by something?" Tommy wracked his brains, trying to call up the image he'd seen. "Like a venomous snake, an insect or maybe some kind of thorn…" His voice trailed off.

The doctor's eyes moved back and forth, as if he was trying to recall some bit of information. Hurrying into his office he punched at the computer console, bringing up the eighteen inch, semi-transparent holographic image of the commander's body. "Search for puncture wounds," he ordered. "Scan for any toxins, or foreign substances throughout his entire system."

The rotating hologram slowed and the right side of his father's body expanded, until it was nothing but the mid-section, just below the ribs. The scraped tissue hid the four puncture marks nicely. A tiny trail led from the surface to the tissue surrounding the liver.

Tommy leaned in closer. "What is it?"

"It is something like the coral you have on Earth, tiny animals living inside minute rocky outcroppings, but on this planet they live on land. They leave a dart, similar to your bees, and in this case the dart will embed itself deep within the victim to release its toxin in a single burst, several hours after the attack."

"And you sent people to live on this planet?" Tommy couldn't believe it.

"They will adapt," the doctor said, his voice devoid of emotion.

"Will my father live?" He kept his eyes on the holographic image, not wanting to see the truth in the doctor's eyes.

A hand came down on Tommy's shoulder and squeezed gently. "If we were to have lost him, it would have been done. He survived the toxin. Had he been alone, rather than with you..." the doctor's voice trailed off.

Tommy swallowed. "Can I see him?"

The doctor nodded.

That was all he needed. Hurrying from the office, he stepped through the particle curtain and moved to his father's side. "He's in stasis?" he asked no one in particular.

"Until the toxin wears off." Mathezar closed his eyes a moment.

Tommy tore his gaze from his father to get a good look at the doctor, who obviously needed to rest before he collapsed. Clearing his throat Tommy spoke just loud enough for the doctor to hear. "Sir, if I may be so bold, should you not be resting as well?"

Dr. Tounga stepped in next to them and leaned in close. "So I have been telling him." He looked from Tommy to Mathezar. "Now if the two of you will get out of my way and let me tend to my patients…" He waved them away, literally pushing them out of the particle curtain to where Jayden stood waiting. "Take them home," he said to her.

They walked in silence towards their quarters. Pausing by Jayden's door, Tommy looked at the doctor. "Please let me know if there's any change."

The doctor nodded. "Rest assured, if there is anything you will be immediately informed." He turned to his daughter. "Come, Jayden."

Stepping into his own quarters, Tommy went straight to his room. He picked up a picture frame from his desk and dropped down onto his bed, staring at the collage of pictures. He smiled at his mother's face, the moments caught on film, the festivals and powwows. A lifetime of events rested in his hand. A lifetime he'd shared with his mother, a lifetime long gone. He wondered what would happen if he was to lose his father as well. Would he consider returning to Earth, to a life that had seemed so much easier?

Slipping into a restless sleep, Tommy found himself back at the scene of the car accident that had claimed his mother's life. Only this time, he stood on the sidelines and watched helplessly as his former self struggled to release the seatbelt. He watched in horror as his mother faded away, while he fumbled with the pendant in an attempt to contact his father.

Chapter 2

Tommy woke a few hours later, still dressed and still holding the picture frame. Passing a hand roughly through his hair, he set the frame onto his desk and hurried from his quarters to medical bay, wanting to check in on his father. He ran down the deserted corridor, barely slowing as he squeezed through the half open medical bay doors. He stopped dead in his tracks when he came face to face with the empty bed pod. There was no particle curtain and no patient in sight. His heart beat wildly as his knees threatened to give out. Where was his father?

"Why are you still up?" Tommy whirled to face Dr.Tounga who stood calmly, digipad in hand. His eyes searched Tommy's face. "Is there something wrong with your father?"

Tommy opened his mouth to speak but couldn't form the words. He didn't understand what was going on. "Where is my father?" he croaked out.

Tounga grimaced. "He should be asleep in his bed."

Tommy shoved past the physician and ran for the door. Dodging the lone crewman in the corridor, he increased his speed as he rounded the last corner. Heart pounding and breathing heavily, he slipped into their quarters and poked his head into his father's room. Empty.

Spinning at the sound of the bathroom door opening, Tommy's jaw dropped as he watched his father, looking as rested as ever, cross the room in a towel.

His father frowned as he took in his son's ragged state. "Did you not sleep last night?"

"Father! What are you doing here?" Tommy could not believe his father stood before him as though nothing had happened.

"Should I be somewhere else?" He frowned, then pointed to his room. "I will dress and join you shortly." His gaze quickly skimmed over Tommy. "I suggest you take a shower before we eat."

Tommy followed his father into his room with his eyes, confused. Letting out a breath he headed towards the shower. Whatever had happened to his father didn't seem to have had any lasting effects on him. Tommy should be happy, relieved, but it wasn't at all how he felt.

When Tommy stepped out of his room, dressed and set for breakfast, his father was standing by the door, ready to exit their quarters. "I wanted to check in on Watoo before starting my day. Would you like to come?"

"Yes." Breakfast could wait. He followed his father down the corridor. "Are you sure you should be on duty today, Father?" Tommy was suspicious of his father's condition, remembering how close he came to losing him last night.

"I see you found him," Tounga said to Tommy with a wry smile as he watched the commander step behind the particle curtain to where Watoo lay.

Tommy furrowed his brows. "Should he be up and about so soon?"

Tounga raised his hands. "If I could have kept him here longer, I would have, but as you can see, it would have been for me rather than for him."

"But he almost died last night." Tommy felt his frustration grow.

Smiling reassuringly, Tounga nodded. "Think of it as though he'd been anesthetised. It would be the best comparison." Pointing toward Watoo's bed, Tounga headed off after the commander.

Taking a deep breath, Tommy clenched his teeth and stepped through to his friend's side. As expected, his friend lay in a regenerative field, but the lower half was dark, blocking his body from view. Tommy moved to the foot of the bed to look over the readouts but he couldn't access the screen. Letting out a breath of frustration he looked up at his father. "Can someone tell me how he's doing?"

"For now we must hold on to the fact that he is alive," Mathezar answered as he stepped into the room. "He suffered extensive damage to his lower body. Even after having regenerated his limbs, there is no guarantee he will ever walk again."

Tommy perked up a bit. "Does that mean he's going to make it?"

The doctor smiled, the kind of smile a parent gives a small child who's about to be told his dog died. "He's alive. He shouldn't be, but he is." Clamping a hand on Tommy's shoulder, the doctor escorted him from behind the curtain. "We'll do everything we can for him."

The commander nodded to the doctor and turned to Tommy. "You are expected in the arboretum this morning. You should hurry if you don't want to be late."

"What?" Tommy stopped dead in his tracks. "Why the arboretum? I didn't even get the schedule yet." The last thing he wanted was to spend the day with Fardoc. Bile rose in his throat.

Ushering his son into the corridor the commander stopped and gave Tommy a once over. "I am not sure what is going on with you, but we will not have time to discuss it until end-of-day meal." He let out a breath, his eyes searching Tommy's. "I have Watoo's schedule. You are expected in the botany lab." He held up a hand to wave off Tommy's protests.

"But school doesn't start for another hour!" Tommy sputtered as his father turned and walked away.

Looking back over his shoulder his father frowned. "You are no longer in school."

Tommy stared in disbelief as his father strode away. He raced back towards his quarters, changed into the proper uniform, downed a glass of juice, and grabbed a muffin to eat on the way to the arboretum. There was no way he was going to face 'Ole Sour Puss' on an empty stomach.

Wiping his hands on his thighs he composed himself before entering the dragon's lair. Why couldn't he be on medical duty with Jayden?

"You're late!" The sharp cry from the one person on the ship Tommy would've liked to avoid startled him.

Tommy looked at the time on the wall panel. "I'm right on time," he protested.

"To be able to start work at 0600 you need to be here a little earlier," he hissed. "Your work detail is posted at your station in the lab." He looked Tommy over in disgust. "And wear a clean uniform tomorrow." With that, he stormed off through the trees.

Dumbfounded Tommy stared down at his uniform. It was clean, well, except for a few muffin crumbs. Sighing, he headed off to the lab. He hoped Fardoc would stay away while he went over his list of duties.

Stepping in to the lab, Tommy paused a moment to look around. He let out a slow whistle as he took in the damage. What had Fardoc been up to? The place looked as though a tornado had ripped through it. Everything had been tossed off the shelves and countertops. Stepping over the broken pots, careful not to step on the plants, Tommy made his way to the lab table. He snorted as he looked at the list of tasks. What Fardoc wanted was a slave, not an assistant.

"Unbelievable," Tommy muttered under his breath.

"Is there a problem?" Fardoc snapped. He stood inches from Tommy. Too close for Tommy's liking.

Tommy drew in a slow breath. "No Sir, I'll get right on this task, Sir." He turned away to hide his look of frustration, grabbed a pair of gloves from the floor and began scooping plants back into their pots. Was this guy mental? Tommy couldn't believe the damage. His father had to see this. Some of these plants were dangerous…what was wrong with him?

Keeping his back to Fardoc as he worked, Tommy waited for the unpleasant excuse of a man to leave so he could alert the commander.

Twenty minutes later, Fardoc was still there, standing over Tommy, watching his every move. Letting out a sigh of frustration, Tommy opened the link to his father.

"Is there a problem?" Fardoc asked, a hint of sarcasm lacing his tone.

Tommy, on his hands and knees, stopped picking up broken shards of planters and turned his head to look over his shoulder. Fardoc's smirk matched his tone. Rage bubbled inside of Tommy, but he forced himself to turn back to his task. He placed the seedlings in a tray and lifted the lot of salvaged plants onto the counter.

"That's not where they go!" Fardoc snapped.

"I was just removing them from the floor, Sir," Tommy said through gritted teeth. He turned back to examine the mess on the floor. He needed more pots but all the others were broken. Grabbing a tray he began laying the plants on it.

"What are you doing?" Fardoc's voice rose to an unpleasant whine.

"What happened here?" The commander's voice barely hid his

surprise.

"What better way to put order than starting from scratch, Commander." The botanist's cocky reply rolled off his lips.

The commander straightened, appearing to grow taller as he held the botanist's regard with controlled fury. "You do realize that some of these plants have taken decades to reach the stage at which they were at? Others are now extinct." He let his gaze slowly pan the room. "We do not tolerate this type of blatant disregard for life…plant, animal or other."

Tommy rose slowly to his feet, laying the tray of plants and seedlings on the counter alongside the last batch. He avoided his father's eyes, wanting to be anywhere but here.

"Take a walk around the arboretum, Thomas," the commander instructed.

Slipping off his gloves, Tommy exited quickly, not wanting to hear what his father had to say. He walked the path that went right to the heart of the arboretum, directly to the trees from Earth. He stopped dead when he found the trees haphazardly dug up and strewn about, some far from their original positions. The stone pathway that had wound through the vegetation was missing, and the bench his father had brought from Earth, from Tommy's home, was nowhere to be seen. "Oh, no…" Tommy's day was not getting any better.

Racing back to his father Tommy barely managed to keep calm as he arrived at the lab. "The bench is gone, Father! The trees have been dug up and moved, everything is a mess."

The commander spun around to face Fardoc. "Confine yourself to your quarters until further notice. I had instructed you to clear any and all changes with me."

"This is my lab; you have no right to tell me how to do my job," Fardoc sputtered.

Tommy was sure his father's eyes flashed red. "Security to the arboretum."

Tommy stiffened. He had only seen the security team once, and they were not to be messed with. Fardoc was headed straight for trouble. Tommy cleared the door as they barrelled into the lab, weapons drawn.

"Escort Fardoc to his quarters," the commander said. "He is to remain there until further notice. He is to have no contact with any of the crew. Outside communications are to be suspended and he is on standard rations until further notice." He rattled off the orders without taking his eyes from Fardoc's.

Tommy had a bad feeling about this. Something was not right, and he wasn't referring to the mess. This guy was dangerous.

As security surrounded Fardoc and ushered him towards the door, the commander held up a hand. "Where is the bench?"

Fardoc shrugged. "Might have been recycled," he said nonchalantly as the guards dragged him from the room.

Moving toward the wall panel the commander typed in some information. A blinking light indicated a spot further down the path from where Tommy had stopped earlier. "Let's go," his father said.

Numb, Tommy followed his father along the wooded path. The arboretum had always provided Tommy with a sense of balance when things got to be more than he could handle. He felt violated, Fardoc's gesture had hit a little too close to home.

As they stepped over a fallen tree Tommy could sense his father's anger at the utter devastation that surrounded them. "Why would someone do this, Father?" Tommy whispered. He felt heartbroken to see plants scattered and tossed into the debris filled pond. The stone pathway and fountain had been torn apart in such a way he wondered if it could ever be repaired.

Grunting as he slammed into his father who had come to a stop, Tommy felt a swirl of anger and sorrow as he examined the strewn pieces of wood that had once been his mother's bench. His father had brought it here so he could have a piece of home; one that carried many memories for them both.

Laying a hand on his son's shoulder, Dthau-Mahsz opened the link and let his energy surround Tommy. "We will repair the bench, Thomas."

Tommy searched his father's face. "And the arboretum?"

Nodding, the commander turned Tommy back toward the way they had come. "Yes. For now, I will have the agricultural team survey the damage and salvage what plants they can."

They made their way down the path, a little slower than before, and by the time they reached the exit, Tommy felt empty. He was missing his home on Earth more and more. "What am I going to do now that the arboretum has been destroyed?" he asked his father.

"Rebuild," his father answered with a look of surprise on his face. "Why would this change your posting?"

Stopping at a door along the school corridor, the commander gestured for Tommy to enter. "What's in here?" Tommy asked. He realized that after being on the ship for three years, he had never been in this particular room.

The lights came on as they crossed the threshold. A conference table surrounded by a dozen chairs sat in the center of the room. Recessed into the far corners were two lounge-like rooms, and a row of computer stations lined the left hand side of the chamber. "This is your classroom, so to speak," his father explained. "You will meet other cadets undergoing specific training in here. This is where you go over your tasks, plan and work out problems, either alone or with the others."

Tommy felt confused. "What am I supposed to do here?"

The commander took a step back and searched his son's face. "You really do not understand, do you?"

The door opened and three cadets entered, talking and laughing before Tommy could answer. "Commander," one of the cadets blurted out, more from surprise than respect and the group stiffened as they came to a halt.

"As you were," the commander instructed. He turned toward a lounge and motioned for Tommy to enter the cozy room. "Sit," he said, a hint of annoyance in his voice.

Tommy walked over to the Spartan sofa and dropped down unceremoniously onto it. His father raised an eyebrow as he sat across from him. "At least these plants are still alive," Tommy remarked, staring at the arrangement in the corner of the room.

Picking up a digipad from the table between them, the commander tapped in a few details before handing it over to Tommy. "This shows you what the arboretum looked like before." A holographic image lifted from the pad and began to slowly rotate. It changed, showing the arboretum's present state of disarray. "This is what it looks like now," the commander shook his head in disgust. "You will redesign the arboretum and implement the work. You will not only participate in the reconstruction, but you will ensure the task is completed as per your specifications.

Tommy dropped the digipad to the table as though it had caught fire. "How can you expect me to do that?" He jumped to his feet and began pacing in circles. "I don't know what to do, where to start."

"Keilah is your mentor, and will assist you with any problems you might have." He drew in a slow, deliberate breath. "You have begun training to assume one of the most important roles in our society. The number of crisis intervention vessels in circulation is determined by the number of commanders we have available." He stood and held Tommy by the shoulders. "Presently, there are only two ships in circulation...the lowest number in over a thousand years."

Tommy took a moment to think about what his father was saying and frowned. "What about when you were with Mom?"

His father sat back in his seat and shook his head, motioning for Tommy to sit. "At the time there were four ships on duty, and it was already difficult to oversee our sister planets' well-being." He passed his hand over his chin. "Which is why it took them so long to find me," his tone softened.

"Were they even looking for you?" Tommy leaned forward, elbows on knees as he bounced a leg nervously.

"No, it was my implant that alerted them to my presence," he said matter-of-factly.

Suppressing a shudder, Tommy rubbed the back of his neck absently. "I still hate the thought of that thing."

"Yes, I am aware of that," his father said dryly. "But we are getting off topic." He braced his hands on his knees and stared directly into Tommy's eyes. "You must learn how every department on this ship functions, down to the last detail. In an emergency, you have to be able to jump in and help out. You have to be sure of the decisions you will be making, because many lives will depend on you."

The weight on Tommy's shoulders suddenly increased and he dropped his eyes. "I don't know if I can do this…" his voice trailed off.

His father stood and straightened his black and blue uniform top. "Today, no. But in time you will assume your place and duty."

Tommy started to rise but Dthau-Mahsz held out a hand. "Take a moment to compose yourself, and then I suggest you begin planning the reconstruction of the arboretum. Those plants are essential to new colonies, as you have seen in the past." He nodded towards the main door. "Keilah is on her way. Discuss it with her."

Eyes lowered, he forced himself to stare at the digipad and let out a slow breath. He heard the door open as his father left, but kept his attention on the holographic image and tried to figure out what to do with the mess.

"You should probably start with a blank slate," a silky voice said.

Tommy stood with a start and stared openly at the person in the doorframe. She was almost as tall as he was, with skin the color of milk chocolate, and electric blue eyes that showed no whites whatsoever. Her panther-black hair cascaded around her shoulders, bouncing slightly as she let out a little laugh.

"I am sorry", she said, smiling sympathetically. "I thought you saw me come in." She bowed slightly. "I am Keilah, daughter of Chei-Szu, and your mentor. I will oversee this phase of your training." She motioned for Tommy to sit. "Please, show me what has caused you so much distress."

He let out a breath of frustration as he took a seat. Pushing the digipad toward her, still displaying the horrid condition of the arboretum, he looked up at her. "I am supposed to fix this," he said sarcastically.

She studied the image a moment before removing it. Calling up another image, she slid the pad closer to Tommy. "There will be times when you will not have the luxury of lamenting over a situation. I suggest you push those feelings aside and focus on the task at hand, before too many plants suffer permanent damage from their ordeal."

Tommy, not sure if he should be insulted, grimaced as he forced himself to stare at the image before him. "It's an empty room." He glanced up at her.

She nodded curtly. "So, then fill it. Redesign it in a way that will allow it to meet all of its duties."

Tilting his head as he considered her words, he began laying the basic groundwork for a path that would separate the different growing zones. He sat back after a while and laughed at the Aztec pattern his paths had created.

Keilah leaned in closer to examine his work. "You find this amusing?"

He shrugged. "Do you think I could create different climates in the arboretum?"

"What did you have in mind?" She shifted in her seat. "Remember that the primary purpose is to have vegetation that can be used in some way. Not just for food, but for building materials, clothing, and medicine." She turned back to face him, studying him openly. "Now, what did you have in mind?"

He tapped on the digipad, increasing the size of his image until it covered the entire surface of the table. "By keeping a uniform climate we are limiting our selection of plants to a certain extent. If we could use a force-field of sorts, to maintain separate environments, then we could benefit from an even greater variety of vegetation."

She nodded slowly, watching as Tommy added vegetation. "What's that?" She pointed to the center of the room.

"I wanted to put the fountain back there, but I thought the tallest trees should have that spot." He moved the virtual fountain off to the side.

"What is this empty area?" Making the area larger, she pushed the sleeves up on her black and tan uniform and leaned in to study it.

He passed a hand through his hair. "I wanted to make a garden, but I wonder if there is a way of growing the vegetables throughout the arboretum, even at the base of certain trees."

Keilah cocked an eyebrow as the corner of her mouth twisted into a smirk. "And what do you know about growing food?"

Tommy sat back and stared at her, not sure if she was mocking him or not. He thought about his answer, about the life he'd led with his mother. They'd grown a huge garden every year, so yeah, he knew quite a bit about growing food. "I have gardened in the past."

Her eyes widened. "Really?" She nodded slowly in approval. "Then that should prove helpful in your planning." She sat back, a hint of scepticism on her face. "You've really grown your own food?"

He let out a discouraged laugh. "Yes, I have." Choosing to ignore her, he returned his attention to the image, resized and began moving plants around again. He changed some of the paths from the harsh straight lines to more of a meandering configuration, figuring the view should always be of nature and not of a plain corridor through trees. Adding a narrow strip of grass and flowers along each side of the path, he then reserved a four foot strip of earth on either side for vegetables, berries and other food bearing plants. He brought some trees closer to the path at random points, set the fountain in the tropical zone and created a pond with a stream that meandered around the room. Adding a few benches throughout the area, he chose a spot with trees similar to home for his bench. He realized with a pang that he hadn't checked on the apple tree Father had taken from the front yard of his home in the Rockies.

Sitting back to take a look at his creation he passed a hand over his tired eyes. He wondered about the acidity of the soil around certain trees and the types of vegetables he should pair them up with. He made a mental note to have the botanical team look into it. Stretching to relieve a kink in his neck he shut his eyes a moment. He was hungry.

"I am impressed with the detail of your project, Thomas," his father said, "but no one said you had to complete it today, or without eating."

Tommy jumped to his feet. Boy was he sore from being hunched over. "I lost track of time." He looked at Keilah, feeling guilty for having kept her through lunch, and ignoring her.

His father laid a hand down on Tommy's shoulder, and nodded towards his mentor, "Thank you, dismissed."

She stood and stretched gracefully. Nodding curtly, she left the room without a word.

The commander picked up the digipad and collapsed the image before handing it back to Tommy. "There is a pocket in the right pant leg, specifically for the digipad. You are expected to have it with you at all times."

The two stepped out into the corridor and headed for their quarters. "I think I'll take a quick shower before end-of-day meal, if that's OK with you, Father." Tommy rubbed at the stiffness in his neck.

His father nodded. "I had planned on eating in the dining hall, but I will admit that I would like to go over your design for the arboretum." He moved aside to let Tommy enter their quarters.

"Could we have them bring us something like the other day?" Tommy asked, pausing by the bathroom door.

The commander seemed to consider the request a moment before he nodded. "Very well, shower and I will send down for our food."

"Sounds great." Tommy hurried into the bathroom, stripped and entered the cylindrical shower. He loved the way the glass walls lit up, how the water flowed from the ring above his head in a stream of varying intensity that covered him from head to toe. He placed his hand on the metal disk imbedded in the shower wall and pivoted until he found the right temperature. Letting out a groan as the water massaged his back, he wondered what was in store for him tomorrow. It had been a rough few days and he could use a break.

Wrapped in a towel, Tommy was greeted by the familiar smells of his mother's cooking as he stepped into the main room. He stopped and frowned. "Is that Mom's vegetable stew?"

"No, well, maybe," his father said with a smile. "Chei-Szu had asked me for the recipe some time ago. It was on the menu tonight." He waved Tommy off. "Hurry and dress so we can eat."

As soon as the meal was finished the two retired to the sitting area, and Tommy handed his father the digipad so he could examine the layout. "This is quite impressive," his father said. "However, you must keep in mind that you will not be working with an empty room." He looked at Tommy for signs of a reaction.

Passing a hand across his face to try and wipe away some of the fatigue, Tommy stared blankly at his creation. "Honestly, I had not yet given any thought as to how I was going to get it done."

His father nodded. "Tomorrow morning when you meet with the team, you will present your idea, listen to their input, make necessary corrections and discuss how to reach your goal." He stood and tugged at his uniform top. "I have to meet with security. I suggest you put that aside and relax a bit if you don't want to spend your night thinking about it." He took two steps toward the door and smiled. "Jayden is here, that should provide a distraction."

Tommy looked over his shoulder toward his father and grimaced. Was everyone taking shots at him today? He watched as the door opened just as Jayden had been approaching. She froze in place and began to fidget. Tommy chuckled under his breath. She still needed time to prepare before facing the commander.

"Jayden," the commander nodded as he stepped out of the room.

Her head dropped as she moved aside. "Sir."

"Come on in, Jayden," Tommy said. "I was just going to call on you."

She made her way around the couch and dropped down in the one across from Tommy. "Gods, I am so tired." She sat up to face him, obviously not that tired. "You would not believe the day I had." She looked around. "Got anything to drink?"

He stood, shaking his head as he went to get some apple juice. His heart sank as he wondered about the state of his apple tree. He'd had a supply of fresh juice since he'd arrived on board because of it. He shook off the negative thoughts and gathered up two glasses.

"You OK?" she asked. "You seem a little off." Her eyes darted over him, giving him a quick assessment.

He snorted. "A little. Did you forget I was spending the day with Fardoc?" He handed her a glass and sat across from her. "So tell me about your day."

She kicked off her boots, tucked one foot under her and readjusted her position. "OK, so it's not as though I've never been in medical bay before, but that's how they treated me! They had me doing the same stuff as Mikah, can you believe it?" She scoffed.

"Hmm, well at least you weren't alone." He thought about his day. "And it's important to cover all subject matter, to make sure you aren't missing any of the basics."

She made a face. "What's wrong with you today?" She looked around the room. "Don't you have any cookies or something to snack on?"

Tommy stared at her in disbelief. Was everyone acting out of sorts today? He stood wearily and went to get a snack. "Didn't you eat?"

She shook her head as she grabbed a couple of cookies from the offered plate. "Gods, no. The last thing I wanted was to be around someone from medical bay."

Unable to hide his reaction, he choked on his cookie. "Your father is the chief medical officer. It's going to be hard to avoid him all rotation."

She scoffed and pointed a finger at him. "Just wait until you have to work with your father." She wiped the back of her hand across her mouth, reached for her glass and downed the last of her juice.

"You won't be able to survive on juice and cookies." He sat back exhausted and watched as she jumped up and moved about the room.

She paused by an end table and picked up the little Ktunaxa figurine, a piece from Tommy's past. He remembered how she'd been drawn to it the first time she'd seen it. "Hey, you didn't tell me how your day went," she said without taking her eyes off the doll. "Do you think you could ask Two-Feathers to get me one the next time you return to Earth?"

Tommy shook his head and stood. He went into his room to get a small wooden box. "He gave this to me two years ago, but made me promise to wait until you asked for it." He handed her the box and watched with curiosity as she opened it.

"It's one of the tribal dancers! How did he know?" She danced around the room happily displaying the tiny figure.

"You're asking how Two-Feathers knew? Seriously?"

"I can't believe you waited all this time to give it to me," she said. A look of confusion crossed her face. "Why did you wait?"

"He said something about.... You know what? I have no clue other than the fact that he made me promise to wait until you asked for it." He turned to go back to the couch but she grabbed his arm.

"Let's go for a walk in the arboretum," she said, pulling him toward the door.

Tommy froze in place. "No." He blurted out harshly.

She stopped dead in her tracks and released his arm. "What do you mean *no*?"

He passed a hand through his hair and tried to come up with an explanation she'd believe. "Look," he hesitated. "It'd be like me asking you to go back and visit medical bay." He didn't need her to freak out over the destruction of her mother's work. He had enough things to deal with right now.

The sound of the door opening cut off her reply. The commander and doctor entered sporting grim faces. Tommy hoped the doctor hadn't planned on telling Jayden the news about the arboretum here. He held his breath and waited.

"Father, Commander," Jayden acknowledged their presence. "Would you like to join us for a walk in the arboretum?"

Tommy cringed inwardly, the commander didn't flinch, but the doctor grew red-faced. "I would rather we returned to our quarters," the doctor answered calmly, despite his flustered appearance. He cleared his throat. "I would like to discuss your performance today."

Good save, Tommy thought.

Jayden spun to face her father, but the commander held up a hand to silence her. "Now is not the time."

She huffed, scooped up her gift from Two-Feathers and took her place at her father's side. Tommy turned away as they left and drew in a deep breath. He dropped down onto the couch, exhausted. He wasn't even sure he wanted to talk to his father about Fardoc, his first day of specific training or what awaited him tomorrow, but he knew his father would have questions.

He'd closed his eyes for only a moment, or so he'd thought. The gentle shaking of his shoulder brought him back to the room. His father stood over him, smiling sympathetically. "If you would prefer going to sleep now, we can talk in the morning."

Tommy sat up and rubbed his eyes. "Actually, I'd sleep better if we got this out of the way. I could use a cup of coffee, though." The impromptu nap had given him time to muddle through some of his thoughts, or so it seemed.

His father laughed. "Join me at the table; I'd like to go over your proposed plan for the arboretum as well."

Tommy stretched and stood to go get his digipad. "Is Mathezar going to tell Jayden about the arboretum tonight?"

His father let out a breath. "He really did not know how to tell her, but the longer he waits, the greater the chance she will find out through someone else. So far the information has been contained…" He looked at Tommy pensively. "I was surprised that you had not told her."

Tommy laughed under his breath. "I'm not suicidal."

"Hmm. Somehow I think the good doctor was hoping you would have."

Tommy looked at his father and they both laughed. "Probably, but then I don't blame him." Reaching for his steaming mug, Tommy inhaled deeply. "I never thought I'd hear myself say 'I need a cup of coffee' and this was only day one."

His father sobered. "Things will not always be this difficult, except for the few times when they will be worse."

"Is that supposed to be reassuring?" He pulled out the digipad and called up his plan. He watched as his father surveyed his work, expanding certain areas as the image rotated. "The idea of growing vegetables between the footpath and trees is interesting."

Tommy shrugged a shoulder. "I'm not even sure it'll work."

His father pressed his lips together as he looked at Tommy. "You'll discuss it with the agricultural and botanical team tomorrow. Together you will come up with a plan of action which will have to be set in motion no later than the next day."

"But that's hardly enough time," Tommy sputtered as he looked at his father in disbelief.

"The longer you wait, the more plants we risk losing," His father said bluntly.

"Yes, but what if I get this wrong? Everything will have to be done over." Tommy shut down the image.

"Then you will do it over." His father drew in a breath. "Before you jump to conclusions, discuss it with your team. Draw on their expertise." The commander picked up their cups and returned them to the replicator. "Enough for tonight. The other topics can wait until morning." He held his son's gaze a moment. "I am proud of the way you handled yourself today. It must have been difficult."

"There's something seriously wrong with that guy," Tommy said, suppressing a shudder.

"Hmm, but unfortunately we cannot dismiss a crewman because of a feeling." His father's tone was grave. "Destroying the arboretum and blatantly disregarding my orders does not help his case."

Tommy shook his head in disbelief. What a day. "Good night, Father." He stood and collected his digipad, hesitated and dropped it back onto the table. "I've had enough for today."

"Good night, Thomas." His father turned and headed for the shower.

Hesitating before entering his room, Tommy turned back and

stared at his digipad. Lips pressed together, he shook his head and went back to retrieve it. Maybe he could go over it one more time before bed.

Chapter 3

"Thomas, are you awake yet?" The commander's voice made its way into the dream Tommy was having. He thought that it was a silly question, since he had been hard at work in the arboretum for hours. Somewhere far away, he heard the door open. "Thomas, wake up."

Tommy opened his eyes slowly and with effort. They felt dry and gritty. "What time is it, Father?" He rolled over and pushed himself up. The digipad slid from his bed to the floor with a thud and a holographic image of the arboretum filled the room.

"You are expected in the main briefing room in twenty minutes to meet with your department heads." His father exited without another comment.

Tommy couldn't tell if his father was angry or not, but right now he didn't have the time or luxury to worry about it. He peeled off yesterday's uniform, pulled on a fresh one, shut the digipad and shoved it in his pocket before running to the bathroom for quick grooming. Five minutes later he was standing by the door, ready to go.

His father, who'd remained seated at the table pointed for Tommy to sit. "Take a few minutes to eat."

If Tommy hadn't been so hungry he would have protested, but his stomach won out. Besides, there was a plate waiting.

Two hours later, Tommy watched as the crewmembers filed out of the conference room. The air buzzed with their energy and excitement for the project ahead. Tommy dropped into a chair and let out a long breath. His father laughed. "You did well. Am I correct in assuming you spent your night researching the compatibility layout for your plants?" His father watched him closely.

Tommy nodded, too tired to move. "Don't know how you do it, Father." He pulled himself up slowly and rubbed his eyes. "I guess I'd better head to the arboretum and get to work."

His father, who'd remained seated, passed a hand over his mouth. "Fardoc will be assisting in the reconstruction."

Adrenaline shot through Tommy and he jumped to his feet, sending his chair flying back against the wall. He planted his hands squarely on the table and leaned forward, ready for a confrontation.

"Sit down, Thomas." His father remained composed. "As unpleasant as it may be, we must deal with our deviant members and do everything we can to reform them."

Tommy shook his head in disgust. He turned around and picked up the chair. "Permission to carry on?"

"Denied." He pointed to the chair. "Sit."

Tommy huffed under his breath and sat down stiffly, avoiding his father's gaze.

"You will come across many situations where you will have to deal with unpleasant individuals. You must remain calm, composed and true to your convictions." A smile tugged at the corner of his mouth. "Remaining calm often unnerves them."

"Permission to carry on, Sir?" Tommy rose and waited for his father's permission to leave, hoping he'd drop the subject. He understood what his father was trying to say, he knew he was right, but he still didn't like it.

"Dismissed."

Head down, Tommy strode towards the arboretum. He *had* been looking forward to the challenge ahead, but knowing Fardoc was going to be there changed everything. He pulled the digipad from his pocket and ran through the list they'd established during the meeting. If all went well, the arboretum would be rebuilt within two weeks. Taking a deep breath he clenched his fists, collected his thoughts and entered the arboretum.

Ten days had passed since the work on the arboretum had commenced and they were down to the planting of the vegetables. A few of the crewmembers were placing benches, rocks, stones, flowers and other items to make the design that much more pleasing. By some stroke of luck, they had managed to keep Jayden out of the arboretum and those who were working on the project had been sworn to secrecy. Tommy laughed to himself. They had been threatened that if they were the ones to leak the news, then they'd have to deal with her outburst. It had worked.

Walking around the perimeter path, Tommy took in the sites. He paused and filled his lungs with the earthy smells he'd always loved. The wild fragrance sparked a sense of well-being that flowed through him. This section definitely meant the most to him, with the different pine, fir and cedar scents mixed in, it carried him back home. He'd had the apple tree brought here along with his bench. He sat down and passed his hands along the worn wooden boards. Memories of so many nights, wrapped in a blanket as he stared up at the stars with his mother flooded back. He indulged in the past momentarily, letting himself drift before he sighed and stood, pushing the memories away. There was still a lot of work to be done.

The vegetation changed as he moved down the path, bringing him to a completely alien environment. He nodded in approval as he made his way into the dense foliage where he came to his pet project, the tropical zone. They had even indulged his desire for a rock cliff and narrow water fall that cascaded into a deep basin. He hoped Jayden would like it.

Satisfied, he headed back to the entrance. It had been a long day, but he'd hoped to be finished within the projected time frame. As he moved closer to the door he saw Fardoc arguing with his security detail. Fists clenched, he walked over to them drawing in a sharp breath to steady his nerves. "Is there a problem?"

Fardoc whirled. "I have been working extra hours every day, and I wish to leave now." The security guards held their position, blocking his path.

"Everyone has been putting in extra hours because of what you did, so I see no reason to let you leave before the others." Tommy surprised himself with his composure. "Carry on," he said as he turned away.

Something hit Tommy hard between the shoulder blades and he stumbled. The sight of Fardoc's smirk ripped all resolve from Tommy. He dove for the botanist and slammed him into the ground. He had the satisfaction of hearing the air rush out of Fardoc's lungs before the security officers pried them apart.

"Thomas!" The commander's voice was sharp, and none too pleased.

Tommy's shoulders sagged. He wasn't sure what was worse, the burning sensation between his shoulder blades, or the frustration at not having had the satisfaction of punching Fardoc's lights out.

"Report." The commander demanded.

"Sir, the chief wanted to be dismissed early and when the cadet refused..." the young security officer started to explain. He swallowed nervously before continuing. "Well, Sir, the botanist threw a rock at the cadet." He pointed to the coconut sized rock before he turned nervously toward his partner. "I wasn't fast enough to stop him." He looked down.

Fardoc sneered.

"Take him to confinement," the commander instructed the security officers. He turned to face Tommy and furrowed a brow. "You are hurt."

Tommy nodded through gritted teeth, but stayed put, not knowing what his father wanted.

"Let us go to medical bay and have Mathezar examine you." He waved Tommy ahead.

With each step Tommy took he felt the searing pain from the impact, offset by the warm trickle of blood as it slid down his back. Light headed by the time he stepped into medical bay, he faltered. His father's firm grip steadied him and Tommy let himself be guided to an exam table.

"Remove your uniform top," his father instructed.

Moving slowly, since every muscle used to perform the task seemed to pass through the impact site, Tommy attempted to remove the top himself. His breath caught as he tugged on a sleeve.

"Hold still," his father said while gingerly pulling on the sleeve.

"I'll do that, Commander," Jayden said cheerfully as she appeared through the particle curtain.

Tommy stiffened. "That won't be necessary." He felt his cheeks heat.

"Thank you Jayden, but I'll handle this." Mathezar stepped in behind Tommy and slid the uniform neatly off Tommy's upper body. "Lie on your stomach, please."

Tommy turned over, placed himself on his stomach with a grunt and found himself staring at Jayden's feet. Well, at least he was still dressed. He closed his eyes and tried not to think about anything. He wished he could have some time off to visit Earth. He didn't even know when the next follow-up visit was scheduled, his father never told him more than he needed to know, which wasn't much.

Jayden moved closer to the table, closer to Tommy, and to his surprise she reached for his hand and squeezed it gently. He found her presence reassuring. "Hold still," she whispered to him.

"I'm almost done," the doctor said. "I have cleaned the wound and removed a bone fragment. The hairline fracture will heal on its own, but you will do nothing for a day or two, then you're on restricted duty for the next two weeks."

Great, Tommy thought sarcastically, just when I was getting into all this. Lately, life just didn't seem to work out for him here. A pang of homesickness settled in his heart. He needed to go for a walk.

Something cold was applied to his back, snatching him from his emotional downward spiral. "There," Mathezar said, "just stop by tomorrow so I can have a look."

Strong hands literally lifted him to his feet as he tried to sit up, and Tommy smiled inwardly at the firm hold his father still had on him. Well, at least the man cared.

"I have to return to the arboretum for a moment," Tommy said. He wanted to make sure everything was in place for the next few days so he didn't have to worry about it. "Besides, I feel fine."

The doctor grunted. "You feel fine because the pain has been numbed, but the effect will wear off sooner if you exert yourself, and I will not exceed the prescribed dosage."

Nodding Tommy turned to face the group. "I just need a few minutes, and then I'll head back to my quarters."

"I'll go with him," Jayden offered. "Besides, I've been anxious to see the changes everyone's been talking about."

An expression of surprise flew between the three men at varying speed.

Jayden laughed. "Oh, come on now. You didn't actually think it was a secret, on this ship?" She tilted her head as she looked from one face to the other. "You did, didn't you?" She grabbed Tommy's arm. "Come on, you don't want to be standing when the meds wear off."

Tommy followed Jayden out, his mind racing. "How long have you known?" He tried to think about what could have given it away.

She looked at him and rolled her eyes as they moved down the corridor. "Seriously? Since you freaked out and refused to take a walk in the arboretum. Besides, it's not like such a horrible thing could be kept a secret..." She paused by the arboretum door. "I just wish you would have told me."

The doors parted and Jayden froze in place, unleashing a smile on Tommy's face. "I have to finish something in the lab and leave a message for the team. Give me a minute, and then I want to show you something." Tommy entered the lab door on the right and Jayden took a few steps down the corridor towards Tommy's new creation.

A few minutes later Jayden poked her head into the lab. "There's something you need to see."

Tommy finished giving his instructions to the AG tech and turned towards Jayden. The smile on his face disappeared quickly when he caught sight of her unreadable expression. His stomach knotted as he followed her from the lab.

She took two steps into the arboretum and paused, biting her lower lip as she cast a glance back at him.

Tommy frowned. "You OK?"

She shook her head and pointed to the domed ceiling, directly behind Tommy.

Earth. The ship was not yet settled into orbit, but the blue marble that grew before their eyes was unmistakable.

All sorts of emotions erupted inside Tommy and he swallowed. Jaw clenched, he kept his eyes riveted to his home. "I need to see my father," he said after a moment. Carried by his torrential thoughts, he left Jayden where she stood and hurried off towards his quarters. He needed some answers.

The commander stood in the living area with his back to the door, probably reading something off a digipad again. "Why didn't you tell me?" Tommy blurted out.

His father turned slowly, obviously considering the question. "I am not in the habit of discussing ship's business with you unless it concerns you."

"How does Earth *not* concern me?"

"Calm yourself, Thomas." The warning in his father's tone was clear. He motioned for Tommy to sit.

Moving around the couch Tommy sat in a huff. The sharp pain from his back reminded him of his injury. "Father, why didn't you tell me?" Tommy watched a strange flicker of emotion cross his father's face, causing Tommy's blood to run cold. "Did something happen?" He knew Earth was on their critical watch list, and that there had been an increase in seismic and volcanic activity. Not to mention abnormal weather patterns, sink holes and even climatic changes that had started around the time Tommy had arrived on board.

Slowly, his father took a seat across from Tommy. "Japan has suffered an earthquake, causing damage to some of their nuclear reactors. The quake set off a tsunami that wiped out Sendai city in Myagi Prefect." He paused. "There have been other incidents of late and we have to evaluate the situation."

Tommy let the information sink in. "I want to go home," he blurted out. "I want to see my friends, Two-Feathers, and the house."

His father held his gaze. "I will not commit to anything until the initial status report is in." The digipad beeped and the commander focused his attention on it. After a long moment, he raised his eyes and stared at his son. "Your increased heart rate has caused the pain relief to wear off." He shook his head, stood and headed for the replicator.

Tommy stared at the floor, not knowing what to think. Could this be it, the beginning of the end for his home planet? He'd sworn to help any way he could…but what could he do? He was nothing more than a cadet, in no position of power. Not to mention the lack of knowledge when it came to emergency situations. He sighed. It wasn't as though he could control the weather or any form of natural disaster.

"Here." His father handed him a blue, marble cup. Warm Durash pulp. Tommy recognized the nutty aroma that rose to greet him. He didn't have a problem with the taste, it was the runny oatmeal texture that put him off, but he knew it would ease the pain he felt, calm his nerves and probably put him to sleep. "Drink. I have a meeting with my department heads, and I promise to wake you if the situation turns critical." The commander cut off Tommy's request before he managed to get a word out. "You are a cadet now, and I will need some time to adjust to your new status." His tone softened. "My primary interest will always be to your safety and well-being."

Tommy nodded, downed the drink in one sip, and stood. The effect was instantaneous. He felt his muscles go slack and his eyelids began to close. His father grabbed his elbow to steady him and escorted him to his room. "I want to go home," Tommy sleepily repeated his primary request. "At least for a little while."

"We will discuss it in the morning." His father un-fastened Tommy's uniform and tugged off his sleeves. Going to his closet, he took a t-shirt and handed it to his son who now sat on his bed in his boxers. Helping Tommy into his t-shirt he lifted him to his feet, slid the covers down from his bed, and steadied him as he crawled into bed face-down.

Tommy awoke feeling groggy. Forgetting about his injury, he tried to sit up. The sharp pain that shot through his back made his breath catch. With a groan he let himself fall back onto the bed and took the time needed to let the pain dissipate. "Time," he muttered through clenched teeth.

"It is 0510," the CPU answered in its detached, male voice.

Tommy turned his head. "Where is my father?"

"The commander is in the briefing room with his department heads."

"Still?" Tommy grunted as he forced himself up. He took out a pair of sweats and slipped on his running shoes, not bothering with socks. He had intended to make his way to the briefing room but each step proved more and more difficult. Relief now being his only priority, he turned into medical bay instead.

Dr. Tounga stepped out of the office and greeted Tommy with a discerning eye. "The pain is intolerable," he stated, then waved him over to an exam table. "Mathezar told me to expect you in the morning, but I am surprised to see you up this early." Sifting through the supply cart, he prepared an analgesic and administered a hypodermic dose to numb the pain. "Give it a moment to take effect, then you can remove your shirt and lie down." Tounga turned and stepped out of the particle curtain and spoke to someone Tommy couldn't see.

The pain receded like a wave returning to the sea and Tommy drew in a long-overdue breath. Easing off his t-shirt, he stretched out, face down on the table, and cradled his head in his folded arms. He closed his eyes and relaxed, revelling in the relief.

Tommy assumed the hand that touched his shoulder belonged to

Tounga, but the reassurance that flowed from it told Tommy his father was now at his side. He kept his eyes closed as the doctor tended to his back, realizing he was in need of some sleep. The bandage must have stuck to the wound, because Tommy could feel tugging and some discomfort as the doctor worked.

"OK, I'm done," Tounga said. "I'm going to help you up."

"No, wait," Tommy protested. "I can do it." He wanted to turn gingerly, in case the shooting pain returned. Sitting himself up, he glanced at his father, not surprised to see how exhausted he looked.

"Hold out your wrist, please," Tounga instructed. Tommy recognized the medipad, a tiny digipad-like device Mathezar had once used on him to filter out a toxin from his system. He watched as the two thin needles were painlessly inserted into the blood vessels of his wrist. Definitely a side to this culture's medicine he appreciated. Tounga affixed the tiny device to the inner side of his wrist and gave Tommy back his arm. "This will make sure you get the pain medication you need," Tounga explained.

Tommy nodded, grateful for the device, and care.

"Let's return to our quarters," the commander said. "There are a few things I need to discuss with you."

Tommy slid from the table and nodded in Tounga's direction. "Thank you, Doctor." Following his father from medical bay, Tommy couldn't help but fear what his father wanted to talk about. His stomach knotted as his imagination ran away with itself, creating scenarios of disaster.

"Wait until I tell you about the situation before you panic,

Thomas." His father said softly. "You should be pleased."

The door to their quarters opened and both men headed for the dining table. "Cantari tea?" his father asked.

Tommy shook his head. "Coffee, please." It wasn't real coffee, just some brew called 'kapou', but the taste was close enough. His stomach growled as he sat himself down.

His father placed a serving of milled garagon seed porridge in front of Tommy and set a plate of mixed fruit in the center of the table. "Here is your coffee," he said as he slid into his seat. Wiping a hand across his red eyes, he forced a smile. "It's been a long night."

"How bad is it?" Tommy asked, referring to the situation on Earth. No sense dragging this out.

"Things seem to have stabilized somewhat. The damage done is done, and now the people are working together to aid one another." He paused to eat a few mouthfuls of his porridge.

"What about the reactors?" Tommy remembered his father saying something about them being damaged.

"Concern over the reactors is high, but our integrity analysis of the damaged structures show that they should be able to handle it. I have a team dispatched to keep watch on them." Picking up his cup he drank slowly from it, staring off into space.

Tommy shrugged and ate while his father worked out his thoughts. Obviously, the commander had something to tell him, but needed to rehash the details. "Do you think we could collect some plants and trees to add to the arboretum?"

His father's eyes showed a hint of surprise. "Which ones did you have in mind?" His full attention had been drawn to his son.

"We don't have any bananas, for one," Tommy started, enthusiasm coloring his voice. "We should have bamboo as well, because it makes good strong wood to build with, it grows fast and in variable climates." He reached for some fruit, turned the piece over in his hand before consuming it. "I'm surprised you don't grow more of the food used on the ship."

His father smiled at his son's enthusiasm.

"I'm serious," Tommy said, insulted.

"Do not take offense," his father said gently. "I am genuinely pleased with your implication."

A moment of drawn out silence settled between the two as they finished eating. "I spoke with Two-Feathers early this morning," his father said. He pushed his bowl aside and reached for the last piece of Shey pod fruit.

Tommy's heart rate kicked up a notch. "Do you think I could visit with him, even if it's only for a couple of hours?" He hoped his father would agree. He hadn't seen Two-Feathers in over a year and he missed the old shaman.

Passing a hand over his mouth, Dthau-Mahsz's amethyst eyes settled on Tommy's. "I am leaving a team behind, and although I am certain you would be safe where you'll be staying, there is still the issue of your injury."

Tommy's heart sank. No… Fardoc could not be the cause of a ruined chance to visit home. "Could Jayden come with me?" He held his breath.

His father cocked his head slightly. "You didn't want to let her see you without your shirt, how could she be of service?"

Tommy felt his face flush. "The trade-off would be worth it."

His father laughed. "Considering I will be leaving an observation team behind, I believe it will be possible, simply because we will be in contact at all times." He pulled out a digipad, verified some information and sobered. "Fair enough. I do like how you appear to have…weighed your options." He stood to clear the table and Tommy followed suit.

Chapter 4

"How long will we be able to stay on Earth, Father?" He was hoping for a few days.

"The team is leaving in fifteen minutes and will be in place anywhere from seven to ten days, so if you intend to go, you should pack. The Phoenix is scheduled to leave orbit in two hours." His father headed for the shower.

"Two hours…Father, wait! Where are you going?" Tommy was confused now. Was there another planet in trouble?

His father paused before turning. His face was neutral but Tommy caught a burst of anger through the link. "I have arranged to transfer Fardoc, now go pack."

Tommy nodded and hurried off, a smile spreading across his face. Pulling his backpack from the closet he reached for his uniform then pulled back with a jerk. "Wow, now that would have been awkward." He took what was left of his *Earth* clothes and shoved them into his pack along with a pair of running shoes. He was too excited to focus.

"You should probably change too," Jayden's voice came from behind him.

He spun around to face her and suppressed a laugh. "You're probably right, but I don't think Two-Feathers would mind." He looked around his room quickly, wondering if he was forgetting anything. "Give me a minute to change out of my uniform; I'll be right with you."

Minutes later, Jayden and Tommy stood in the yard of the two-story farm house that had belonged to his great grandparents. Tommy paused to slowly take in the sights, to admire the mature trees, generously cast about the land. The sun had past mid-point in the clear blue sky, casting shadows through the leaves. How he'd missed the majestic Rocky Mountains. Tommy filled his lungs with the fresh mountain air, trying to memorize the invigorating pine and cedar scents carried on the summer breeze.

"When you two are done sniffing the air, come inside." Two-Feathers called out from the porch. He stood there in his jeans and chambray shirt, looking exactly the way he did the last time Tommy had seen him.

The sight of his old friend filled Tommy with a flood of warmth. He was glad, and somewhat relieved, to note how strong and healthy Two-Feathers appeared to be. He dreaded the day he would lose his friend.

Jayden dropped her bags and ran straight into the shaman's open arms. Tommy had to see it with his own eyes to believe it. *Maybe Jayden would be better off here as well*, he thought to himself. Tightening the grip on his bag, he stooped down stiffly to pick up Jayden's bundle and started slowly towards the house. He let his mind flood with the memories and feelings of a lifetime. He was home. His heart swelled in his chest and his eyes stung as he made his way up the porch steps.

Without saying a word, the old shaman drew Tommy into a hug, careful not to touch his injury. "You told me you wouldn't stay away so long. I'm not getting any younger, you know," Two-Feathers said solemnly.

Tommy smiled as he swallowed a mix of emotions. He let the smell of incense and fresh washed cotton surround him, comfort him, before stepping back with a nod.

Jayden poked her head into the porch to grab her bag. "Your room will be upstairs, the same one you used last time," Two-Feathers said in his gravelly voice.

Tommy reached for his pack but the old shaman was quicker. "Your father told me not to let you do anything for the first two days, and then he made a list of what you could and couldn't do afterwards."

"What?" Tommy sputtered, "What do you mean 'what I could and couldn't do'?"

"You would have had the same conditions apply had you remained onboard," the commander said from behind Tommy. He stepped forward to greet Two-Feathers heartily.

"Rest assured, Dthau-Mahsz, they will be in good hands." Two-Feathers reached into the pack at his hip and pulled out a small leather pouch. "Grey Wolf said to give this to you. He wants you to promise to wear it at all times until you return for these two. He said you would know what to do with it when the time came." He reached forward and slipped it over the commander's head.

To Tommy's surprise, his father tucked the pouch inside his uniform top. He made a mental note to question Grey Wolf about it later. He wondered nervously about the vision the seer had had this time.

"I must take my leave of you; we are due to break orbit shortly." The commander turned, revealing a few packages on the floor behind him. He handed the first one to Jayden. "Your father packed this so you can perform your duty as med-tech, Cadet." He shot Tommy a look of warning, and Tommy nodded with a sigh. "As per your request," the commander said with a smile as he handed the biggest box to Two-Feathers.

Grinning, the old shaman left with the box, tugging on Jayden's sleeve for her to follow.

"This is for you," the commander said as he held out a wrist com. "I was surprised that you did not bring it on your own. You do realize the observation team does not have a telephone to check in on you." The corner of his mouth betrayed the teasing. He placed the thin metal band around Tommy's outstretched wrist and pulled his son into a hug. "Enjoy your stay, my son." He stepped back and searched Tommy's face. "I hope you can find the peace you search for."

Tommy held his father's gaze. He'd never mentioned anything to his father about how he'd been feeling, but as usual, he didn't have to. Now he regretted not having taken the time to talk to him about it. He watched as his father's form silently vanished.

"You coming?" Jayden called from the kitchen.

Shaking his head as he made his way to the kitchen, Tommy paused to look down the hallway toward the living room. He wondered if two-Feathers had made any changes, but he didn't feel right about wandering through the house on his own. This was no longer his home; it had belonged to Two-Feathers for three years now.

"OK, I think I have all the vegetables we need," Jayden was saying as she rummaged through the fridge. She closed the door and settled at the counter with a paring knife.

Two-Feathers was mixing something at the stove, nodding. "You just going to stand there?" he said to Tommy.

Tommy shook his head. "I think I'm going to go out to the barn."

Two-Feathers paused to look at him, pointing with the spoon he held. "No chores."

"No chores."

Two-Feathers reached for a few carrots and gave them to Tommy. "This should buy you some forgiveness."

"I'll check your bandage after end-of-d– after supper," Jayden added.

"Hmm." Tommy headed back outside and crossed the yard to the barn. He paused when he saw that Two-Feathers had replaced the apple tree, which now grew in the arboretum, with a young chokecherry tree. The yard looked whole again and it felt as though he had stepped back in time. Memories of his mother working in the garden while he chopped wood, or sharing a meal out on the porch together came back to him…but that was a lifetime ago. He sighed, letting the images fade.

A flood of warm air, laden with the scent of hay and horses, engulfed him when he opened the barn door, magically lifting his spirits. He just stood there, eyes closed and inhaled deeply, taking in all the smells while listening to the sounds of life within. After a few moments he approached Thunder, slowly, wondering if the horse would remember him. He walked to the stall and stared into the big brown eyes. Holding out a carrot, he reached over to rub the soft nose while the horse ate. Tension left Tommy's body and a lazy smile spread across his face as he talked softly to Thunder. God, he'd missed this.

After making his way to each of the animals, right down to the chickens, Tommy headed back to the house. The sun had dropped behind the mountains, and the faint glow from the kitchen window welcomed him. Quietly, he entered the house through the mud room, just off the kitchen, and washed his hands. He listened to the easy chit chat between Jayden and Two-Feathers. No one on board would believe how different she was when she was here. Life seemed so much simpler here.

"Good, supper is almost ready," Two-Feathers said. "I know ship time is off with our time, but you look like you could use a good night's sleep."

"I'm almost tempted to pitch a tent and sleep outside," Tommy answered. He moved to get the plates and utensils but was met with a disapproving look from Jayden. "I'm quite capable of setting the table." He ignored her and laid out the dinnerware.

"Why did Grey Wolf give a medicine pouch to my father?" Tommy blurted out in the middle of the meal. He'd been lost in thought while Jayden chewed Two-Feathers' ear off.

Jayden fell silent, waiting for the old shaman to answer.

"He didn't say anything to me other than to make sure your father had it on him at all times," he answered slowly. He laid his hands on either side of his plate and looked into Tommy's eyes. "I stopped asking a long time ago, just as you have learned not to question me anymore."

Not the answer Tommy was hoping for, but he couldn't say he was surprised. Two

-Feathers was right, those who knew him no longer asked 'why', they simply trusted his wisdom and followed his guidance.

Jayden snorted, drawing everyone's eyes. "What?" She shrugged. "I can't imagine not demanding answers, never mind simply not asking." She shook her head incredulously.

"In time, you too will become wise," Two-Feathers offered, causing Tommy to choke on his mouthful.

"You don't believe him?" Jayden asked, more hurt than insulted.

Tommy put his fork down and reached out to touch her arm. "I have seen changes come over you no one on the ship would believe. He just took me by surprise." He gave her arm a squeeze then withdrew his hand. Leaning back in his chair he pushed away his plate, feeling drained. "I don't mean to be rude, but I think I should call it a night." He stood and picked up his half eaten plate, depositing it beside the sink. Fatigue, mixed with a mess of emotions had drained him. He'd find time to talk with Two-Feathers later on.

He made his way up the stairs to his old room, his old bed, and it was like stepping back in time. He wasn't sure it was a good thing since it only added to the confusion he felt in his heart and in his mind. Kicking off his boots without undressing, he stretched out face down on his bed, an arm hanging off the edge of the mattress. Within seconds, he was asleep.

Dawn was barely breaking when Tommy awoke. From the position he was in he probably hadn't moved all night. Staring out his window, he watched the darkened sky grow brighter, and listened as the night sounds were slowly replaced by the awakening world. Crisp morning air had filled his room and he drew in a deep breath. The air on the ship never felt or smelled like this.

His movement unleashed a burst of pain through his back. He gritted his teeth and pushed himself up onto his knees to sit. Stiffly, he stripped off the clothes he'd slept in and rummaged through his pack to find jeans and a t-shirt which he donned with a smile. It felt good to be home.

As he turned to open his door he noticed a blue chambray shirt with the Kutenai logo embroidered on the front pocket. The gift from Two-Feathers touched him. He reached for it and pulled it on over his t-shirt before making his way quietly down the stairs. Cold seeped through his socks when he stepped out onto the porch, but rather than go back inside, he settled down on an old rocker, mindful of his back, and crossed his arms against the chill in the air. He listened as the animals in the barn woke with the morning and let himself remember the past.

"Here." Two-Feathers offered Tommy a steaming cup and settled in a chair beside him. He eyed Tommy without turning to face him. "Fits nice."

Tommy smiled and took a sip from his cup. Hot chocolate from his father, something Two-Feathers really liked. "Thank you, for the shirt and the cacao."

The shaman nodded and continued to stare out at the mountain peaks, visible above the tree line.

"Are you worried?" Tommy didn't clarify his question, technically he wasn't allowed to. Well, there was that and the fact that his father had told him not to say anything.

He took a sip from his cup and inhaled deeply before turning to face Tommy. His expression was so peaceful, as though there was nothing to worry about, as if he knew some secret that promised to keep him safe. "There is nothing to be troubled about. No matter what, man will continue."

Tommy shook his head. "I've seen devastation, both man-made and from natural causes, and I've assisted in the transfer of colonies."

"And because of your actions, these people will continue." His dark eyes held Tommy's. "You must have faith in Great Spirit's plan for Mother Earth."

Tommy let out a sigh.

"That goes for you as well," Two-Feathers said. "Trust that you are on the right path."

Tilting his head he searched the old shaman's face. "I don't know where my place is, and I don't seem to fit in anywhere anymore," Tommy said glumly.

A look of amusement filled the dark eyes. "I remember having a similar conversation with your mother many years ago."

"What do you mean? Mom loved this place." Tommy got his love of the Rockies, of nature and animals from his mother.

He laughed under his breath. "By the time you showed up, yes, she loved this place, but when she'd first arrived after the death of her parents, it was to close up and sell the farm."

Tommy shook his head. "I can't imagine Mom even thinking of selling this place."

Two-Feathers nodded. "Coming home brought things into a different light. She had been very active in the city as both a nurse and a teacher, but there was something missing from her life. Something she found when she came home." He paused for a sip from his cup.

"What does that mean for me? Am I just supposed to let fate push me into my place?" He felt discouraged and didn't try to hide it.

"Sometimes you have to stop paddling and let the current carry you. In the end, you will end up where you were meant to be. You can either show up refreshed and ready to face life, or exhausted from trying to get away from it." He nodded slowly. "It's time to ride the current."

Tommy threw his head back and winced. "That's not helping...it doesn't tell me if my place is here on Earth, or with my father in space."

"Hmm. Tell me, knowing what you know now, could you return to Earth and act as a simple citizen? You would be all but helpless to make a difference or prevent what is still to come." He stood and handed Tommy their cups. "I will tend to the animals, then make breakfast. Give yourself a break and don't think about anything today, just enjoy yourself." He walked down the steps and headed to the barn.

Jayden poked her head out the door and looked around. She watched Two-Feathers make his way to the barn before bringing her attention back to Tommy. Her face lit when her eyes settled on him. "There you are. I was worried when I saw that your room was empty."

He pursed his lips. "Worried I was out mucking stalls?"

She tilted her head but continued without missing a beat. "You're very funny. Now, are you coming in so I can dress your wound? You fell asleep before I could tend to it yesterday and I will have to explain that, so please help me..." She let her voice trail off, a half tortured smile on her lips.

Tommy remembered the look his father had shot him before leaving. Jaw clenched, he stood and headed back inside to the kitchen. "We can do it here," he said. He hung his shirt on the chair next to him and tugged off his t-shirt with a grimace. It still hurt to move his arms above his head.

"I can help," Jayden offered.

He held up a hand. "You will be helping in just a second." He turned a chair, straddled it, and rested his head on his arms so she could tend to his injury. Her touch was light, but he jumped anyway.

"Did I hurt you?" Concern filled her voice.

He shook his head without looking up, afraid she'd see the color that tinged his cheeks. "Why is it taking so long to heal anyway? It can't be worse than a scrape." He tilted his head to the side to watch her.

She finished laying out the pack the commander had given her, and looked over at him with a frown. "You were hit with a bandoo nut. Not all the spines have come out yet."

"Security said I'd been hit with a rock. Why would such a thing be lying around the arboretum?" Tommy remembered the specimen that grew in the botany lab. It was a short tree with a wide, green trunk and palm like leaves that grew one grey nut at a time. The nut could easily have been mistaken for a rock, but like some form of cacti, it had very short, fine spines covering its entire surface. Tommy felt some satisfaction knowing Fardoc must have quite a few embedded in his hands.

"Trust me, it wasn't a rock, now hold still." Her touch was surprisingly clinical as she worked. "I have a few more to remove before I can dress it again." She laid a hand on his shoulder. "You OK?"

He nodded, trying not to think about anything. He wasn't ready for the sharp tugging, worse than having hairs yanked out and let out a yelp.

"Sorry, the longer they stay in the more they tend to take root."

He jerked back. "What? That's disgusting, take them all out!"

Two-Feathers came in with the egg basket and bucket of milk. Quickly washing his hands, he leaned over Tommy for a look as Jayden yanked on another spine.

Tommy jumped. "Ow! OK, never mind, leave them in."

"Wait," Two-Feathers said. "Just give me a minute." He turned away and rummaged through his herb cupboard, placing several jars on the counter. With a mortar and pestle he ground up his mixture and prepared a poultice while Jayden looked on. He handed the finished product to Jayden. "Apply this to his wound and wait twenty minutes; it should draw the spines out."

Jayden worked meticulously, spreading the mixture while Tommy visibly relaxed. "How does that feel?" she asked.

Tommy shrugged a shoulder. "I don't know, cold."

"Hmm. OK, I'll wait."

The welcome smell of breakfast cooking filled the room, and Tommy relaxed as he listened to the sounds of his friends working around him. Jayden's touch, though gentle, startled him. "I'm sorry," she said. "I thought you were still awake. I'm going to remove the poultice and withdraw the spines now."

Tommy relaxed back onto his folded arms to let her work. Two-Feathers stepped in to mutter something to Jayden, and he felt the shaman's strong hands move over his wound. Tommy braced for the worse, but before he knew it, and without the earlier discomfort, they were done. "Get dressed and go wash up," the old shaman said. "It's time to eat."

A few days later, on a wooden pier that jutted out into the lake, Tommy sat in the warmth of the sun. He watched as Jayden played with his friends in the water, splashing and laughing. He couldn't believe she had never been in a lake before, or that she didn't know how to swim.

Every time Tommy decided his place was with his father, something showed him all he was giving up on Earth. Growing up sucks, he decided.

"You gonna sit there all day or join us?" Mike shouted out to him as he dunked Will in the lake.

His friend would have died three years ago if it hadn't been for Mathezar and his intervention. No, Tommy couldn't turn his back on all that life in his father's world had to offer, even if it meant not hanging out at the lake. It was time to grow up.

Peter dropped down beside Tommy without taking his eyes off what was going on in the water. "Hey," he said tentatively.

"Wanna talk about it?"

Tommy exhaled sharply. "Not much to talk about," he lied.

Turning slowly, Peter's grey eyes searched Tommy's. "You can trust us, you know, and you can drop the BS."

Tilting his head without breaking eye contact, Tommy furrowed his brows. "Where'd that come from?"

"Look, it didn't take a genius to figure out that Mike should have died if not for what your father did. He told us about the dream he had." He turned away from Tommy. "You disappear for months if not a year at a time, somewhere where you can't even Skype or email us." He smiled as he watched the others in the water a moment before he brought his gaze back to Tommy. "Since when does the military allow kids to tag along, anyway?"

Pressing his lips together Tommy let out a slow breath, a sharp contrast from the high speed chase his mind was involved in as he tried to come up with an explanation.

"Hey, don't bother answering if you're going to lie," Peter said sharply.

Tommy cringed inwardly. "I wish I could tell you. I really want to..." his voice trailed off.

"It's not like I'm asking you to show me around your space ship," he said with a straight face.

Stiffening, Tommy held his breath, unsure of how to react. Time seemed to crawl to a stop.

Peter burst out laughing. "You win man. You looked so serious, I almost believed you." He stood and left a wet bathing suit mark on the pier's sun-bleached planks. "Come on, let's go swim too." A mischievous grin spread across his face as he nodded towards the end of the pier. "Race you." Without waiting for an answer he was off.

Tommy jumped to his feet and scrambled after Peter, catching up to him as they reached the end of the pier and they leapt into the air above the water simultaneously.

Deciding last minute to tuck his legs into a bomb he let himself sink into the water unceremoniously. A rush of tiny bubbles streamed around Tommy's body as the cool water engulfed him. Relishing in the feel of the bubbles he allowed himself to float slowly back up to the top.

Jayden's touch startled him as his head broke the surface to draw in a breath. He sputtered, but gave her a forced smile when he saw the look of concern on her face. "*I* can swim, remember?" A rush of warmth flowed through his chest where her hand had touched him. He reached for it and gave it a reassuring squeeze. "You shouldn't be out this far," Tommy said with some concern. He nodded towards shore. "Come on, let's swim in closer."

She gave him a sheepish look. "I just wanted to come see you. You looked a little lost out there." Water droplets glistened on her eyelashes and the sun gave her skin a healthy glow, drawing his attention to the details of her face.

He felt a strange flutter in the pit of his stomach and was unable to take his eyes off of her. "I'm fine," he croaked out. "Now show me what a good swimmer you are and let's head back to shore."

Her legs brushed against his as she turned and started back towards the others. Tommy didn't miss the tingly feeling that lingered, but as Jayden swallowed a mouthful of water he snapped back to the present and moved alongside her, guiding her back to shore.

As the group toweled off, they tossed around suggestions for the evening. "Could we roast marshmallows?" Jayden asked.

Mike nodded. "We can pick up stuff from the grocery store before it closes." He checked his watch. "Going to have to hustle though. "Where are we doing this?"

"We can stay here and sleep out under the stars," Peter suggested.

Tommy half-nodded in agreement. "Makes sense, this way we won't have to worry about driving home late," Tommy offered.

Will scoffed. "When did you become so responsible?" he said in a teasing tone.

"We could head back to our place," Jayden offered timidly.

Tommy studied her closely. He could sense that she was nervous about staying out here all night. Not wanting to embarrass her he shot her a quick reassuring smile and turned back to Will. "Since we didn't bring anything to spend the night I think we should just head back home and hang there." His tone was nonchalant, but he secretly hoped the guys wouldn't tease Jayden for being afraid to sleep outdoors, since her only experience had been the time they were stranded in an alien colony with nothing but his survival skills to rely on.

Tommy tapped the wrist com nervously. The last time he'd been given one it'd had a direct link to his father. This time he'd had no answer, from anyone. He tried again, and spoke to the thin black band. "Phoenix observation team, this is Cadet Thomas, please come in."

"Observation outpost Sol III, go ahead cadet," a commanding female voice filled the room.

"Did you receive any instructions as to when we would be leaving?" Tommy asked. A nervous band constricted his chest.

"Negative, we are on standby."

"Shouldn't we have been picked up by now?" Tommy hoped to get a some information.

"You will be contacted when the time comes, cadet." The voice softened somewhat. "Is there anything else?"

"Yes, ma'am, there is. Could you tell me what your observations show?" His voice trembled slightly. "Will we have to intervene?"

There was a pause. "The commander will be the one to make that call. We are here to observe and collect information."

Tommy felt his frustration build. He was in no mood for a run around. "There must be something you can tell me…you've been collecting information for days."

"You will be informed when the others are informed, cadet." The voice took on a sharper tone. "I am not at liberty to discuss details with cadets, unless they are on rotation with us. Is that clear?"

"Yes, ma'am." Tommy sighed and tossed the band across the room. He turned to walk out of his room, then stopped, let out a breath of frustration and went to retrieve the thin black strip. He still needed it.

Furious, he stormed down the steps and headed outside, letting the porch door slam shut behind him. "Still no news?" Two-Feathers asked from his perch on the railing.

Tommy shut his eyes and clenched his jaw as he exhaled sharply. He took a moment before he lifted his eyes to meet the shaman's and shook his head. "No."

Two-Feathers nodded, stood and motioned for Tommy to sit on the bench. He made his way to the rocker next to Tommy. "Ready to tell me what's on your mind? You've been moping since you got here, so I'm going to guess you still haven't decided where you belong."

Tilting his head to stare at Two-Feathers he let out a surprised chuckle. He could no more hide anything from his father than he could from Two-Feathers. He shrugged, feeling disheartened. "I don't seem to fit in anywhere." He jammed his hand through his hair.

The old shaman smiled affectionately. "No one just fits in. You have to make your place, and just because it seems easy for some, does not mean it is."

"If Mom hadn't died," he started, but Two-Feathers held up a hand.

"You would still have been faced with this decision. Your parents had an agreement." He stopped rocking and leaned forward, bracing his hands on his knees. "You cannot deny your heritage. Sooner or later, a choice will have to be made."

Tommy let his cheeks puff as he blew out a breath. "What if mom had followed my father?"

He shook his head slowly. "Then you would be back here to check out Earth, to see what you might miss out on or have to leave behind."

Letting his head roll back against the siding of the house, Tommy considered Two-Feathers' words.

"It isn't easy to accept that from one day to the next you have all these responsibilities, or that all of a sudden people expect things of you." He paused.

Anger flashed through Tommy. That wasn't it, he wanted to yell. But as the words sank in he realised that maybe, just maybe, Two-Feathers was right. Maybe he didn't want anyone to have any expectations of him. He had failed his mother and she'd died right there beside him…he never wanted to have that kind of responsibility again. He wanted to be left alone.

"How's your back?" the old shaman asked, changing the subject.

"I can barely feel it anymore."

"And with time, this will no longer cause you any discomfort either." Bracing his hands on his knees, he rose. "Perhaps you should enjoy what time you have left here. Who knows, maybe one day you won't be able to return."

The sound of gravel sputtering under a truck's tires caught Tommy's attention and he waited for the vehicle in question to appear through the trees at the end of the driveway. Mike's bright red pick-up truck emerged and he honked when he spotted Tommy sitting on the porch. The sound of the screen door slamming told him Jayden had joined him as well.

Lowering his window as he slowed the truck to a stop by the stairs, Mike poked his dark head out the window. "Feel like hitting the drive-in tonight?"

"It's cheapy Wednesday," Will called out from the passenger side.

Jayden looked at Tommy, eyes wide. When he nodded curtly she called back, "Yes!" Her enthusiasm made the boys smile. She moved closer to Tommy. "What's a drive-in?" She asked in a hushed voice.

Tommy laughed and stood. "Give us a minute to grab a few things," he said to Mike.

"Are the others coming too?" Jayden asked.

Mike nodded. "Jason and Peter have a ballgame tonight, so we'll pick them up on the way."

Tommy ushered her into the house and towards the stairs. "Grab us each a sweater and take the blanket from the mudroom," he instructed. "I'll get some stuff for snacks."

Minutes later, they were on their way down the mountain in

Mike's truck. Tommy had barely had a moment to try to explain what a drive-in or a movie was to Jayden. Out of frustration, he had ended up pushing her out the door, telling her to go with it.

Jayden shifted and leaned on Tommy's shoulder, she'd fallen asleep minutes after they'd left the drive-in, stuffed full of cotton candy and popcorn. Tommy looked down and at how her hair cascaded over her face in her sleep and resisted the urge to sweep it away. He had spent more time watching Jayden tonight than the movie. He smiled to himself as he thought about how insistent she'd been for them to stay for the second movie.

"You still in school?" Mike asked.

Tommy drew in a slow breath, and brought his attention to Mike. "Yeah, but it's more like work-study than just school work." He figured that this would be the best way to explain it. "You?" He tossed the question back.

"I decided to take a year off school to work." Mike kept his attention on the road as he answered.

Tommy could hear the hesitation in Mike's voice, and wondered if Grey Wolf, his father, had reacted badly to the news. Mike had always been really good in school and was sure he'd go on to university. "Your dad OK with that decision?"

Mike shrugged. "I didn't know what I wanted to study, so I decided to take a step back and give myself some time." He looked at Tommy and flashed a half-hearted grin. "My mother didn't take it well at first, but my dad backed me." He shrugged with one shoulder. "I couldn't imagine myself wasting a year trying classes. My folks worked hard for the money they saved for my education. I want to be sure of myself."

Tommy nodded slowly, absorbing the information. "What about the rest of you guys?"

Peter sat up in the passenger seat and turned back to face Tommy. "I leave for Vancouver in August."

"UBC?" Tommy asked.

"Yeah, looking at a bachelor's in Earth and Ocean science," Peter said. "Would have preferred the Okanagan Campus, but they didn't offer it."

"School's not for me," Will said sleepily from beside Tommy.

Jason snorted from between Mike and Peter. "He's gonna hustle his way to the top." He tried to look over his shoulder at Tommy. "Before you ask, I work with my old man in construction. No clue if it's just for now or forever, but I like it."

Tommy let the information sink in. Only Peter seemed to know where he was headed. Tommy found some reassurance in knowing he wasn't alone in his feelings of uncertainty, and just maybe, he was normal. He leaned back against the seat and let his mind wander for the rest of the trip.

Chapter 5

Twelve days had come and gone, yet there was no sign of the Phoenix. Last night, visions haunted Tommy and he couldn't help but wonder what was going on. He had already contacted the observation team twice, but they had not received any feedback from the Phoenix either. The sky was light now, and soon the sun would rise. Tommy needed to talk with Two-Feathers, or even better, Grey Wolf. Maybe the seer had had some visions as well.

Voices from the kitchen caught Tommy's attention. Was Grey Wolf here this early? Two-Feathers hadn't mentioned anything. As he moved down the hall in his pyjama bottoms he recognized the voice. Relief flooded through him. It wasn't Grey Wolf, but Mathezar. His father must be with the doctor. Hurrying to the kitchen Tommy stopped dead when he caught the grim expression on the doctor's face. Tommy swallowed the dry lump in his throat. "What happened to him?" His insides began shaking. "Is he OK?"

The doctor shifted in his chair to face Tommy and forced a smile. "He is stable."

"What happened to him?" Tommy repeated the question. "Where is he?"

Two-Feathers motioned for Tommy to sit.

"I don't want to sit; I want to know what's going on." He felt like throwing up.

"Getting upset won't help. Sit down and listen to what the doctor has to say so we can act accordingly." Two-Feathers pulled out a chair for Tommy. "Please, continue Doctor."

Taking a deep breath, the doctor began to speak slowly, almost as though he had to think about every word. "The Aurora is standing by to rendez-vous with the Phoenix, who is, as we speak, retrieving your father from the Osiris. We are to meet up with them as soon as possible." The doctor paused, watching as Tommy absorbed the information.

"My father is not with you?"

"No." The doctor's voice was low, calm.

"Well, what about the observation team? We don't all fit in the Aurora." Tommy was confused. "And that doesn't tell me what happened to my father."

The doctor shook his head. "We are not sure what happened to your father. I don't have any information other than he is now in stable condition."

Tommy slammed his fist down onto the table. "Does this have anything to do with Fardoc?"

The shaman rose and went to the stove for some hot water. He opened the cupboard and retrieved a little jar from which he spooned some of its contents into the steaming cup of water. He set the brew down in front of Tommy without a word and sat back in his chair.

"Thomas," the doctor said in his best fatherly tone. "We have no information other than that he is alive." He shook his head and furrowed his brows. "What are you getting through the link?"

Tommy sat back, surprised. Aside from the visions, he hadn't felt anything out of the ordinary through the link. "What should I have felt?"

Mathezar pressed his lips together. "Well, you are still young, but the bond you and your father share is quite strong, so even from this distance you would have known had he died." His voice faltered.

Tommy let out a long, slow breath, then reached for the cup Two-Feathers had given him. Taking a sip, he grimaced, forcing himself to swallow the foul concoction and waited for the onset of relief. Eyes closed, he let his mind drift, reach out. He tried to consciously contact his father. The signal was very faint, but it was there, giving Tommy some relief.

"What did you sense?" Two-Feathers asked.

Tommy shook his head. "I'm not sure, but if I had to guess I'd say he's alive. It's almost as though he was asleep, or unconscious." His voice dropped off.

"If he had died, you would have felt it," Jayden said from the doorway. "I was with Father when Mother died..." She turned away from the doorway. "I saw what it did to him," she whispered.

Tommy remembered what his father had said about having felt his mother die in the car accident, that neither time nor space could prevent such a feeling from coming across. "When did it happen?" he asked the doctor.

"Unfortunately, only your father will be able to give us the details. He did not make the rendez-vous. We were able to locate him because of the tracking chip." The doctor reached across the table for the coffee pot and refilled his cup.

Jayden set out a plate of muffins, scones and jam in the middle of the table before settling herself between her father and Tommy.

"What I don't understand is why you're here and not with my father?" Tommy's tone was almost accusatory.

"He's not the one flying the ship!" Jayden snapped.

Tommy felt his face flush. "I'm sorry, Doctor, I'm just worried about my father."

The doctor nodded. "We are all worried." He cleared his throat. "The observation team left three days ago. It was decided that until your father was found, we would leave you where you would be safe."

"The others left? When are we leaving?" Tommy stood and paced nervously. "Why are we still here, now?"

The doctor exchanged glances with Two-Feathers, who nodded slowly, urging the doctor on. "Very well," the doctor started. "The Aurora was found adrift just outside the solar system, no one onboard."

"But you just said it was standing by," Tommy said.

"The Atlantis left with the observation team, and a pilot has remained behind to bring us back to the Phoenix, but we had to be sure you would be safe first."

Tommy frowned, turned to face the doctor and leaned back

against the counter. "You keep saying that, but safe from what, exactly?"

The doctor looked stunned. "You have amethyst eyes. You are the only one born of a parent with amethyst eyes." He passed his hand through his hair.

"You're serious." He looked at their faces, one by one and shook his head. "This is ridiculous." He walked out of the kitchen.

"Where are you going?" Jayden called after him.

"To finish packing." He muttered as he stomped off and up the stairs.

Less than ten minutes later he was back with both his and Jayden's packs.

"Good," said Two-Feathers, "now come eat. Who knows how long it'll be before you have a decent meal again."

Jayden pointed to a bag on the counter. "I'm bringing supplies. I hate those rations we had to eat the first time we came here."

Tommy nodded in agreement, but said nothing. "Was the shuttle checked out before it was brought here, or did you lead the 'bad guys' right to me?"

Two-Feathers looked at him with a raised eyebrow. "Be nice," he warned.

"Meaning what," Mathezar asked, unable to hide his curiosity.

"Well I don't want you to take this the wrong way," Tommy started. "But you don't seem to be the tactical type when it comes to warding off an attack." He accepted a plate with a large helping of a cheese and vegetable omelette. "How do you know the ship isn't bugged?"

"Bugged?" both Jayden and Mathezar said in unison.

Tommy took a bite of his eggs and waved his fork around while he tried to explain. "You know, planted a tracking chip or something on it." He grabbed a scone from the middle of the table. "Hey! It's still warm!" He looked at Two-Feathers. "My father let you have dishes?"

"One," the old shaman said nonchalantly. "I eat alone most of the time, so it's nice."

Tommy shook his head in disbelief. Now was not the time to get off topic. "Think about it," he said to the doctor. "Who is this pilot? How long has he been part of the crew? Are we sure we can trust him?" He paused for a sip of coffee. "Is the shuttle safe and how sure are you we won't be ambushed on our way home?"

Feeling suddenly awkward, he stopped talking and stared at the three sets of eyes fixed on him. "Was it something I said?" He felt his face flush and looked down. OK, maybe he was ranting, but these people didn't seem to have a clue when it came to enemy attacks and such.

"Your analysis is quite impressive," the commander said, stepping into the kitchen.

"Father!" Tommy started to stand but his father stopped him.

He took a seat next to Two-Feathers who immediately got up and poured a cup of water. Everyone knew what that meant.

Tommy scrutinized his father closely. Except for looking as though he hadn't slept since they'd separated, he looked fine and his eyes were intact. Tentatively, Tommy made contact through the link. *I was worried, Father. Are you sure you're OK?*

Very tired, my son, but all is well. I had to know you were unharmed. He accepted the cup from Two-Feathers and sniffed cautiously. An eyebrow went up but he drank deeply from the stoneware mug, much to everyone's surprise.

Tommy watched the doctor out of the corner of his eye as he pulled a digipad from his pant leg and began to check the commander out himself.

"I am fine," the commander reassured the good doctor, and everyone else. "I am exhausted and looking forward to some sleep, but I had to make sure you made it back safely." He held Tommy's gaze. "And you were right, Thomas. The other shuttle had been a trap. He emptied his cup, pushed back from the table and stood.

Everyone else followed suit.

"I am sorry to have to leave so quickly, Two-Feathers, but –"

Two-Feathers held up a hand. "I appreciate the visit, A-kiss-no-haus tsa-a-nam."

Jayden shot Tommy a look, but Tommy just mouthed 'later' to her. He let out a huff at the face she made. "It means *star-brother*," he said just loud enough for her to hear.

"For the next while, they should be more frequent," the commander said. "At least until things settle down here." He turned back to the group. "We must quickly take our leave."

Jayden hugged the shaman tightly, and then said something to him that made him laugh. She made her way back to the counter and scooped up her care package.

When it was Tommy's turn he held tight to the old shaman, hoping to see him one more time. "I'm not done watching you grow up," Two-Feathers said with a strained smile. "If you don't mind, I'll stay here and clean up. You just go on now, and be safe."

Tommy nodded, wiping back the tears with the heel of his palm. He swallowed hard then made his way to the living room to where the others waited.

Once onboard the doctor moved in rapidly, attempting to escort the commander to medical bay. "I am going to my quarters, dear friend," the commander said. "I need a shower, some food and I intend to sleep."

Tommy shot a glance in the doctor's direction, not sure what to do. His father seemed fine, but was obviously exhausted, and he was sure that had Mathezar detected anything abnormal with his scans his father would already be in medical bay.

Following his father into their quarters, Tommy watched as he headed straight for the shower. Tommy reached out through the link, not wanting to pry, but needing to make contact, to know for sure that his father was OK.

While he waited for his father to come out of the bathroom, Tommy prepared a bowl of hearty vegetable stew and a cup of Two-Feathers' warm brew. Sniffing it tentatively, he was surprised by the pleasing aroma. Anything he'd ever had from Two-Feathers had tasted terrible. He put the cup down and went into his room to get a pair of track pants and a jersey for his father.

"I brought you some clothes, Father," Tommy said from outside the door.

"You may bring it in," his father said through the door.

Tommy stepped into the room holding the bundle. "I brought you some of my clothes that are loose fitting…" his voice trailed off as he spotted the mottled bruises on his father's back. Without taking his eyes from his father's injuries, he laid the garments on a small cabinet by the door. Regaining his composure he changed the subject. "I set out some stew for you, if you're hungry." He dropped his eyes as his father turned to face him, not knowing what to say.

"Thank you." He pulled the shirt over his head and followed Tommy to the table. He laid a hand on Tommy's shoulder. "I am fine," he said as he eased himself into a chair, barely hiding a grunt. He closed his eyes a moment before starting to eat, focusing on his food.

Tommy went to get himself something to drink and came back to his father, figuring his father would let him know what happened in time. "Let me help you to your room, Father," Tommy said as he watched his father struggle to stay awake.

"Forgive me. I know you would have liked to discuss what happened since you left for Earth, but I need to rest first." He stood shakily, and reached for his plate.

"Leave it, Father. I'll clean up." He watched his father move toward his room, and fought the urge to help him. "I wanted to take a quick look at the work done in the arboretum, but if you prefer I stay here..." Tommy said before his father entered his room.

He turned to face Tommy, forcing a slight smile. "I will be fine. I expect the good doctor to show up any minute now, so you can tend to your duties."

"You are more important, Father." He paused, no longer sure of his decision as he watched his father move towards his room. "I could stay, in case you needed something. My visit could wait until tomorrow.

"Go."

"I will be back soon," he said as the door closed behind his father.

The door chime rang and the doctor entered uninvited. He stopped short when he saw Tommy. "Forgive my intrusion; I wanted to check on the commander."

Tommy pointed toward his father's door. "I'll be back shortly."

Mathezar nodded, and Tommy headed off to the arboretum, not surprised to find Jayden waiting for him. "I was hoping to see you," she said. She was still wearing jeans and a pale green sweatshirt, with the sleeves pushed up to her elbows. Tommy liked the tan hiking boots and the braids she wore.

"I wanted to check on the progress in the arboretum," he explained.

"Me too."

He eyed her suspiciously.

"I'm serious." She hooked an arm around his elbow as they

walked. "I barely got to see it since you started the renovations."

He exhaled sharply. "Forced renovations." He stepped aside to let her enter first. "Let's just walk around the perimeter; I don't want to leave my father alone for too long."

"He's not alone," she said as she skipped ahead. "Come on, I want to see the tropical zone." A spark of mischief flashed in her eyes. "I'll race you," she said as she sprinted off through the winding path.

Tommy shook his head and followed. "You are going the wrong way!" he called out to her. He chased after her as she made her way through the trees and avoided the path. "Stop!" he called out in warning. "Watch out for the thorns!"

"Hey! What is all this?" she called out, just out of sight. "Ow!"

"Don't move, I'm right behind you." Tommy caught sight of her and made his way through the shrubs, avoiding the long thorns on the trees. He looked around for something to push away the menacing outcropping. Using a branch from the ground he pushed the long prickly branch out of the way, clearing a path for Jayden. "Here, step out now."

"Gods! Why would you have such plants?" She pushed a lock of hair from her eyes.

"They grow fantastic fruit, and that's one of the reasons we have paths, by the way." He offered a hand to steady her.

She looked at the branch he held in his hand. "I can't believe the crew left such a branch on the ground."

"I told them to leave some of the debris to nourish the soil." He tossed the branch back down. "Now what exactly did you want to see?"

The sound of people talking caught their attention. Jayden tugged at his arm and dropped down behind some shrubs. "Shh," she hushed him when he started to protest.

The crewmembers grew nearer. "...all I know is that the commander has returned. The doctor is tending to him now," a man's voice said.

"Do you think Fardoc attacked him?" a woman asked.

"No, I heard it was the Binari," another man said.

"Oh, come on. They defeated them years ago," the woman retorted.

The group passed Tommy and Jayden, oblivious to their presence. The teens held still as the crunching of the boots continued along the path.

"Then why would the boy have been sent off-ship around the time the commander just happened to get attacked?" the first man asked.

Jayden rolled her eyes, and Tommy pressed his lips together, trying not to laugh at all the drama.

"The Binari had been on their quest for almost four hundred years," the second man continued. "You don't just give up on something like that."

The group continued to walk and talk, unsuspecting. Once they moved out of earshot Tommy stood and pulled Jayden to her feet. "I can't believe they'd spread rumors like that," Jayden commented.

Tommy choked back a laugh. "Aren't you the one filling everyone in on the 'latest news'?" He pulled her back towards the entrance. "I'd like to check in on my father, and this rumor."

"Sure. Somehow I knew my visit would have to wait, but leave the rumor investigation to me." The corner of her mouth curled up and Tommy shook his head.

"You're terrible." He eyed her appreciatively. She could be a handful, but well worth it in the end, since she was a good friend. He leaned in close, looking to the left and right before speaking. "You'd blend in more if you'd change, I think you'll stick out in your terran apparel," he whispered.

She swatted him on his arm, her face turning to a pout. "I like my new clothes." She looked down, admiring her boots. "I think I'm quite fashionable."

He burst out laughing and ushered her out the door into the corridor. His eyes locked on hers, holding her gaze. She challenged him, tilting her chin. "What?" she asked.

He pressed his lips together, stifling his smile and winked. "You're one of us now...I think you've crossed over." He expected to get swatted again, but her expression changed, taking on a more serious look.

"You may be right." She tugged on his sleeve, leading him down the corridor. "Come on, I've got some information to scrounge up."

They walked back to Tommy's quarters in silence. He could no longer deny that the feelings he had for her were growing, changing. This complicated things more than he liked, but right now he had his father to deal with. He still had no information on the attack and the rumor about the Binari left a sinking feeling in the pit of his stomach.

"I'm going to change so I can blend in," she said teasingly, pulling him from his thoughts.

"Let me know what you find."

She smiled. "I'll be back soon enough. Let me know how your father is." She turned to head for her door, but stopped to fix one of the plants in the hall.

Tommy watched, debating if he should tease her about it but decided to let it drop. He took a deep breath and entered his quarters, coming face to face with the doctor and his father, sitting across from one another on the couches. He shot a look at the doctor. "Shouldn't he be in bed?"

"You may address me directly," his father snapped back. He obviously did not get any sleep.

Tommy sighed. "Would you like me to help you to your room Father?" He watched his father shift uncomfortably in his seat.

The doctor shook his head in warning, but it came too late.

"Thomas, both you and the doctor will do me the pleasure of letting me tend to my personal needs, on my own." His father stressed the last three words.

"Yes, Father." Something was definitely off. He looked from his father to the doctor. "Was I interrupting anything? I could come back later…" He felt uneasy, but held his ground as he watched the strange exchange between the two. His father reached for the cup on the table but set it back down when he realized it was empty. "Would you like more?" Tommy offered.

His father closed his eyes, clenched his jaw but to Tommy's surprise, nodded.

The doctor stood and collected his effects, his expression blank. "If you need me I shall be in medical bay." The statement was directed more at Tommy than his father.

Reaching for his father's cup, Tommy followed the doctor back to the door. "Thank you for coming, Doctor." He watched the door close behind the doctor and sniffed the contents of his father's cup. Farou tonic. Strange that it was in a cup and not in a glass. Tommy refilled the cup, walked back to the sitting area to give it to him, but then rather than join his father, Tommy drifted towards the port hole to watch the stars.

Life had been so much easier growing up, and he longed for that life again, but this time Earth's very existence was threatened. Taking social or political action to help was one thing, but there wasn't much you could do against volcanoes, earthquakes and tsunamis. Lost in thought, he was taken aback when an unexpected wave of stress assaulted him. He turned to see his father, half asleep on the couch, stir and realize where he was.

"I am sorry, Thomas, I had not realized that I..." His father paused, struggling for control.

The wave of stress dropped and dissipated, but Tommy knew

his father was only hiding it. Shaking his head, he stepped away from the port hole and sat across from his father. Seeing the tension that had appeared around his father's amethyst eyes worried him, since his father had always managed to remain calm, even in the worst situations.

"What's wrong, Father?" Reality hit. For the commander to lose control of his side of the link was even more alarming than the uncontrolled stress that had come from him. Tommy immediately opened his side of the link, allowing his father to draw from his own energy.

His father forced a smile, but thankfully Tommy felt him draw on the offered energy. Reaching shakily for his cup, the commander downed its contents, set the cup back down on the solid wood table and dropped his head into his hands.

Clenching his jaw, Tommy watched his father. A series of images flashed through his mind and he gasped, feeling his blood turn to ice. "So it's true," he said, not needing confirmation. "They are back."

His father looked up and furrowed his brows as he studied Tommy. "What did you see?" The question came from the commander within him, all business and no room for negotiation.

Tommy hesitated. "I saw the Binari, with another victim..." his voice trailed off. He suppressed a shudder. "How is that possible?" He still had the occasional nightmare about the Binari and his narrow escape from death, about his father's slow recovery and the feelings of helplessness.

His father's eyes were sharp as he watched his son. "How could you see those images? I had closed the link." He pressed his lips together. "Perhaps not soon enough..."

"They just popped into my head, but there are already rumors circulating throughout the ship," Tommy said truthfully. The only time he had ever 'seen' anything was through the link when his father had granted him access, so how come he had not only seen, but felt these horrible images? He wondered just how injured his father was for his control of the link to be compromised...

"I had not planned on sharing that information with you just yet," his father cut into his thoughts, passing a hand across his chin. He drew in a long breath and Tommy watched the transformation that came over his father as the Farou tonic kicked in.

"I don't understand. We had destroyed their leader and the necklace. Why would they try again?" Bile rose in his throat. "Did this have anything to do with Fardoc?"

"I want to say no, but I am beginning to wonder," his father seemed willing to share information now.

Tommy's mind raced, there were too many things that didn't make sense. He rubbed his hands on his jeans and tried to come up with probable scenarios. "Where did Fardoc come from? I mean, we'd been without a chief botanist for three years, and yet the crew had handled things fine. We didn't need anyone." Tommy rattled off his thoughts, not waiting for an answer. "Did you even bother to check him out?"

His father tilted his head. "Enlighten me, please. What do you mean by 'check him out'?"

Tommy stared at his father. "On Earth, if some specialist would have shown up out of the blue to take over a job, people would have asked to see his papers. They would probably check references, confirm with someone higher up that he'd really been sent to do the job." He passed a hand over his mouth. There were just some things about this culture that didn't make sense.

"Send full data report on Fardoc to my digipad," his father called out to the CPU.

"Any information you have on him, and Dohn-Mar," Tommy added. He let out a sigh of frustration. "Doesn't it seem strange that the last time we had dealings with them it started with incidents onboard?"

"Please explain, because none of this makes any sense."

Tommy clenched his jaw. "OK, Creighton –Dohn-Mahr's son, was openly hostile to me because of my mixed bloodline. He had been influenced by his father's beliefs, and although you did not share all the information around the Binari's attempt on me while on Earth, you let enough information slip for me to assume Dohn-Mar had been involved." He sat on the edge of the couch, leaning closer to his father.

"Go on." His father's gaze never left his.

"Doesn't it strike you as odd, that the second someone shows up exhibiting some form of hostile behaviour, one of us gets attacked? Not once, but twice." He stood to pace the room, racking his brains for some tiny bit of information. "I have never come across any type of hostility from your people."

"Our," his father corrected.

Tommy nodded and waved a hand. "Yes, *our*, but do you understand what I am trying to get at?"

The digipad beeped, drawing both sets of amethyst eyes to it. Tommy moved to his father's side and sat down, straining to read off the pad as his father quickly skimmed through the information. Releasing a breath of frustration the commander handed the pad to Tommy. "You were right."

Tommy frowned. "Father?"

"Both Dohn-Mar and Fardoc had openly and repeatedly displayed violent behaviour. The two had received treatment from the same center, at the same time. Neither Dohn-Mar nor Fardoc originated from Sirius…they should have never been part of this crew," his father went silent. "How could we have been so blind?"

"Maybe you've never had to be weary of those around you in the past." Tommy pressed his lips together, wondering if he dared suggest it. Taking a deep breath, he pushed on. "Maybe you should run a check on all crewmembers. You know, just to be safe."

After a moment of thought his father reached for the digipad and tapped away at it. Tommy managed to sit in silence as his father worked for all of five minutes. Jumping to his feet he went for his own digipad, maybe it was time he followed a few hunches of his own.

He made his way back to the common area, eyes focused on the readout. Onboard this ship, no other reports of violence had been filed, but when Tommy tried to look up other ships he found that his access was quite limited. He'd have to ask his father to check. OK, but maybe he could check on any new additions to the crew, as well as any crewmembers from other planets.

"Access denied," the screen repeated the message. Tommy tossed the pad off to the side, and stormed off to get a drink. He'd rather be running, horseback riding, sleeping or anything other than wasting his time.

His father's eyebrows shot up. Tommy could feel his father's eyes on him as he made his way to the replicator. He turned to see his father reach for his pad and scroll through the list. "All you had to do was ask," his father said.

Tommy frowned as he swallowed his last sip of juice. "Ask for what? Access to top secret information?"

His father laughed. "You were trying to access information through your school digipad."

"And that's funny?" He was frustrated with the limitations imposed on the 'youth' of this society.

"Where is your digipad? The one you used to plan the arboretum." His father waited, keeping his attention on Tommy.

"I only have one…" he paused, frowning. Going back to his room, Tommy took his uniform from the edge of his bed, where he'd tossed it before he'd left the ship. Patting down the pant leg he felt the digipad, pulled it out of the pocket and headed back to the common room. It was only side by side that he noticed the subtle differences in the two pads. He looked up at his father who dutifully handed his pad over to Tommy with a slight smile. "Do all the adults have one like yours?"

"No," his father laughed. "This one is unique. Each department head has the next closest thing and so forth."

Tommy blinked, trying to grasp the implication behind such a structure. "Does that mean information is withheld from people because of their function?" Implants, information control, this was not a good thing…

"Thomas. You are able to access the same information through all the 'adult' digipads as you put it. Where they differ is in their ability to call up personal information. Each department head has access to pertinent information on their staff, I have access to information on all my crewmembers…I have just never used it." The bitterness in his voice slipped out.

Tommy let out a breath. "OK, that says a lot about this world. Unfortunately, mine has a much darker side to it." He thought about the crew. There wasn't much in the way of rotation so he knew or had at least met everyone onboard. "Who's that new guy in security? He looks a little different, so maybe he's not from your planet either." Tommy had dealt with him when Fardoc had first been detained, and once when their paths crossed during endurance training. "I don't think he's displayed any violent behavior so far."

"I will check him out," his father said. "But now I must get some sleep before the good doctor finds me here and forces me to miss the next two days." He stood and nodded towards Tommy before making his way to his room.

"Sleep well, Father." Tommy bit down on his lower lip. Well, that was strange, he thought as he watched his father disappear into his room. Maybe he could do some investigating of his own while his father slept. He reached for his father's digipad and asked for a list of all crewmembers, hoping his father wouldn't be too mad at the intrusion.

The door chime sounded and Tommy dropped the pad. His heart raced in his chest as he made his way to the door. He expected Jayden with her tidbits, but took a step back when he saw the doctor. Oh, now he understood. He clenched his jaw, suppressing a smile at his father's quick escape. "Doctor, come in."

Tommy stepped aside and watched as the doctor went straight for his father's room. He wondered if his father would be playing possum.

Jayden poked her head in. "Can I come in too? I have a few things to talk to you about," she said in a low voice.

Tommy waved her in. Shooting a glance over his shoulder, he pointed to his bedroom door and ushered her in. He went back to the sitting area and grabbed both his and his father's digipads, leaving the useless school one behind.

As the door to his bedroom closed behind him, he felt a strange twinge of discomfort. It was almost as if he was doing something wrong, and it had nothing to do with the fact that he had his father's digipad.

Jayden sat at the edge of his bed, so Tommy grabbed his desk chair, flipped it around and straddled it. "What did you find out?"

"OK, we've been gone two weeks, right? Well there's a new security guard –."

Tommy cut her off. "I met him before we left."

She held up a hand. "Let me finish, please, and I wasn't talking about T'inau. I was referring to people who have come aboard while we were away."

Tommy frowned. Reaching for his father's digipad he called up a list of all ship's personnel. He turned the pad towards Jayden. "I don't know what you've heard, but according to this, no one has come aboard since Fardoc arrived."

Jayden grabbed the pad. "This is wrong."

"That's impossible." Tommy tapped on the edge of the pad. "This is my father's digipad...the *commander's* digipad."

"Well it's wrong." She chewed at the corner of her mouth. "Hold on, I'll be right back." She jumped to her feet and left his room without explaining. Less than a minute later she returned holding yet another digipad.

"If you took the one off the common room table, it's useless." He watched as she shook her head, keeping her focus on the pad.

"Here, look." She held the two lists side by side. "This is father's digipad, and as chief medical officer he has to have all personal information on every person and crewmember onboard." She laid the two digipads on the bed. "Where's yours?"

Tommy pointed behind him. "On the desk, why?"

She grabbed his digipad and placed it next to the commander's. The list, as it appeared on the commander's pad was copied into Tommy's. She then repeated the process with the doctor's pad. "OK, be right back." She scurried from the room and was back not a moment later, only to leave with the commander's digipad.

"OK," she said, closing the door behind her. "I transferred the data from both pads to your own. Now let's have a look." Grinning triumphantly, she turned the pad over to show Tommy what it said. "There are four new crewmembers. Unlisted on your father's list, but not on mine."

"That doesn't make sense."

"Actually, it does. Your father lost his digipad in the attack. This list is from his new one, a planted one, obviously." She stared at him, seemingly proud of herself.

"What's with you?" He eyed her curiously.

She pressed her lips together, attempting to suppress a grin, but it lit up her whole face, bringing a mischievous twinkle to her eyes. He couldn't help but smile and shake his head. "You do know that this is not a Nancy Drew mystery." She'd engrossed herself in his mother's book collection while on Earth, spending hours reading every chance she got.

She lifted her chin. "Mock me if you must, but there are things going on here…"

He settled back in his chair and reached for the digipad to study it. "All this shows is that there are four people missing from my father's list." He looked at the doctor's information. "I don't understand why your father has this info."

She shook her head. "The CPU does it automatically when you bring someone onboard. Their info has to be added to my father's data base in case they are carrying some sort of malady or have special medical requirements." She held his gaze. "When they snuck your friend Mike onboard, there is a listing of that here as well." She tapped on the screen.

He was surprised at the revelation, but then, all those who had assisted in his care knew about his presence.

"Hey," she said as she touched his arm. "With all the transfers and such, my father often shows up with someone requiring medical attention. He is brought onboard, treated and returned to his or her planet, never to come back here again."

"Do we have any info on these four new crewmembers?" He tried to look for something, but in reality, none of it made much sense.

"Here." She pointed to a common link. "They all carry this enzyme."

Tommy made a face. "I wasn't talking about their medical history." He shoved his fingers through his hair and sighed, he thought she was on to something.

"You don't get it, do you," her tone was cautious. Again, she pointed to the common link. "You can only get this if you are exposed to the food on Trygus III." She waved her hand as she launched into an explanation. "If you don't have this enzyme, you will be poisoned by the food. Trygus III is a warrior planet. They think nothing of people dying from their food, claiming that the weak have no place in the universe, but if you eat a certain combination of plants, your body develops the necessary physiological changes to adapt."

"Stop, I still don't get it."

Her face flushed. "Sorry, ignore the medical side, and focus on the warrior side."

Tommy's expression became serious. "Warrior?"

She nodded. "Uh huh, usually up for hire."

He wasn't sure what to think. Had the Binari hired people to resume their quest? "Does it say where these people were born?"

She scanned the results a moment then Tommy watched as her brows furrowed. "This can't be…" her voice trailed off as she called up more information. "Three of them have no ties to Sirius."

"Meaning what?" Things weren't getting any clearer.

She made a face, a sure sign her patience was waning. "No one is allowed to work on this vessel unless they are direct descendants of the Guardians."

Now he was really lost. "Guardians?"

"Us!" She shifted around and Tommy saw a flash of anger in her eyes. "The Forefathers left us, the descendants of the very first planet seeded, in charge of the sister colonies. Don't tell me you didn't know that!"

He felt his cheeks flush at the crack. "I didn't grow up here. I knew the story; I had just never heard the name *Guardians* before." He thought about that a moment. Then he remembered Petra, the pixie-like medical aide and Chei-Szu with his electric blue eyes that had no whites. "Are you telling me everyone on this ship came from the planet Sirius?"

"No, some crewmembers were born either off-world or in space, but their parents were born on Sirius. And for the children of those born in space to one day be part of our legacy, they must return to Sirius to have their own children."

They sat in silence as Tommy digested that bit of information. "But I was born on Earth."

She nodded. "Yes, but your father was born on our home planet. And *yes,* every member of the crew is Sirian." She watched him wrestle with the information. "What is it that causes you to doubt?"

He stood and took a few steps. "Well come on, Jayden. Petra and Chei-Szu look nothing like you or my father." He turned to face her, settling a hip on the edge of his desk. Tommy watched as Jayden's expression went from surprise to amusement before she broke into full blown laughter. He crossed his arms, insulted. He had no idea what could possibly be so amusing.

"Have you looked at the diversity on your planet?" She bent over and continued laughing.

He shook his head, not getting into the mood, which only seemed to increase her laughter.

The door slid open and both fathers stood in the doorway, taking in the scene. Tommy was grateful he'd been sitting on his desk, even if his father frowned upon his doing so. Jayden regained some composure but flat out ignored the two men and continued to giggle to herself.

"Ignore her," Tommy said. "She's laughing at me."

"Time to go, Jayden," the doctor said hesitantly, "...unless the two of you were working on something for school."

Tommy shook his head, stepped out of his room and went to the sitting area, followed by the rest of the group. His gaze settled on his father. "Are you feeling better?"

His father nodded, but Tommy caught the bulge in his jaw line as he clenched his teeth. Apparently, things were not fine there either.

"I'll call on you later," Jayden said to Tommy as she made her way to the door.

The doctor exchanged glances with Tommy's father, but the commander held up a hand to ward off any comments. Nodding, the doctor left in silence.

It'd been almost an hour since the doctor had left with Jayden, yet Tommy and his father had not said a single word to one another. Surprisingly, the silence was comfortable, letting Tommy delve into possible plots and scenarios. Tommy had hoped his father wouldn't question him about what he and Jayden had been discussing, but it seemed as though his father had things on his mind as well.

"What happened to Fardoc?" Tommy asked. He was trying to figure out if he'd had any connection to the four mysterious crewmembers.

His father's eyes honed in on him. The hand resting on his chin slid slowly away. "I was told he died in the attack."

"But you don't believe it." It wasn't a question.

"No."

Chapter 6

Tommy made his way anxiously to medical bay, having promised to be there when Watoo was released. He had visited his friend often since his accident, and more so since he'd regained consciousness. It had taken weeks for his legs to regenerate and just as much time for Watoo to get back on his feet, but Tommy had helped in every way he could. Watoo had been reluctant to let Tommy visit at first, but over time he accepted the company.

Unfortunately, Tommy's rotation in medical bay wasn't to start for another three days. Three days after his friend's release. Jayden would be assigned to Watoo for the next rotation, something Tommy would have liked. After having expressed this desire to his father, his father had only nodded, saying he understood how Tommy felt, but the schedule was what it was.

"Wait for me!" Jayden ran up to him from behind. She was wearing her jeans, hiking boots and the tan chambray shirt Two-Feathers had given her.

Tommy frowned. "Why are you wearing that?" He had to admit, having her hair tied into two braids made her look cute. The corner of Tommy's lip curled upwards. *Cute, as long as she doesn't open her mouth,* he thought.

She shrugged, looking down at herself. "For the next two days I can wear what I want, so why not?"

"OK, but then you're missing the concho and feathers," he said, referring to the decorations Two-Feathers always wore in his hair. He grabbed her by the sleeve and tugged her forward. "We have to hurry if we don't want to miss Watoo."

She stopped dead and her sleeve snapped out of his grip. "He was released last night and is in his quarters resting."

Tommy whirled around. "What are you talking about? He told me he was to be released this morning." He didn't believe her.

"No." She shook her head with a confused look on her face. "I was there when Father released him. I thought you were going back to the arboretum." She shifted her weight onto one leg and put her hand on her hip.

Tommy searched her eyes. "You're sure about that?"

"Yes, he left on his own." She waved down the corridor. "Can we go to the arboretum now?"

He scratched his head and dropped his hands to his sides, disappointed. "I've seen enough of the arboretum to last me a while." Maybe Watoo just needed to be alone.

It was her turn to drag him along. "Today, you get to visit as a tourist," she said with a smile.

"I don't know Jayden, I'm not really in the mood."

Her smile disappeared and she yanked him closer. "I need to talk to you, so play along," she whispered in an urgent tone.

Tommy nodded slowly. "Look, I'm just disappointed I didn't get to help Watoo settle back into his quarters, and I'm starving."

He motioned for her to follow him back to his quarters. He wanted to get his note pad and pencil so they could communicate without being heard or using their digipads.

"OK, but I want a snack too." She followed him into his quarters.

He laughed under his breath and headed back towards his room. "Do you know what you'll be doing with Watoo this rotation?" He grabbed his notebook and pencil from his desk and slipped them into his pant leg pocket, then returned to the dining area to grab two muffins from the table. "Here," he said as he handed her a banana chocolate chip muffin and stepped back into the corridor. "Come on."

She took a huge bite of muffin and let out a sound of pleasure.

"Don't tell me you're still avoiding meals with your father." He had never met such a stubborn person, ever. "You haven't answered my question."

She swallowed and brushed a crumb from her chin. "About my rotation with Watoo, right?"

He nodded. "Yeah. I mean, will you be doing school work or colony transfer prep?"

She shoved her hand down the front of her shirt and pulled out her digipad, popped the last of her muffin into her mouth and began consulting her pad. Tommy stared in disbelief. "What? These pants don't have pockets that are big enough for my digipad." She returned her attention to the information on her pad. "Classroom prep, ugh. I was sure I was going to be going planet-side."

Tommy couldn't suppress the laugh that her rotation sparked. It was kind of like sending a shark into the kiddy pool and expecting everyone to play nice. He dodged her hand as she attempted to swat him. He raised a finger at her. "Careful, physical violence is frowned upon."

She dropped her head, trying to hide the pink rising in her cheeks, and Tommy pretended he didn't see it. "I'm not sure I get this rotation thing," he admitted. "I thought we were going to have 'specific training'. I mean, how specific is it if we have to go through every department?"

Jayden's eyes widened. "Do you really have rotations in every department?"

Tommy frowned. "Yeah, why? Don't you?" He tried to recall what he had seen of Jayden's schedule.

"No. I have botany; both on and off ship, medical, and teaching, if you can believe that."

Tommy forced out a breath. "Well you have been practicing on me for years now."

She tilted her head. "That's where it came from. I mean botany and medical is obvious." She skipped on ahead and entered the arboretum.

Tommy hurried up to her and grabbed her by the arm, turning her to face him. "But what do you really want to do?" He was still uneasy about the imposed role each person was to assume in this society.

Jayden lifted one shoulder into a shrug. "I'm not sure. I had thought I'd be more interested in botany, but I really enjoyed my medical rotation."

"After all the fuss you made throughout your rotation?" He really didn't get her at times.

Mischief colored her eyes. "Well, if he thought I hated it, then he wouldn't expect a great performance. It kind of takes some of the pressure off." She pushed past him and stepped onto the stone path that led them to the heart of the arboretum.

"Hmm, I suppose that's one way of looking at it." He followed a few steps behind her, so he could watch her reaction as she passed through the bushes and flowers.

"Do you really have a rotation in every department?" She spoke as she made her way to the center of the pod. When she came to the densest part of the arboretum she stopped and looked at him. "Where'd you put your mother's bench?"

"I'll show you that later. Come see this." He pulled her to the biggest tree in the arboretum. "This is from my home on Earth." He stepped up to the giant's trunk and pressed his hands lovingly against the bark. "It's a giant redwood tree, and it is hundreds of years old." He looked at her and smiled. "Come on, sit here with me." Nestling onto the ground, in a niche made by the large roots, he held out a hand for Jayden to join him. With their backs pressed against the trunk, knees bent, they settled against the majestic tree.

"I can't believe you took this from its forest, especially if it's as old as you say," she said, looking into his eyes, and lingering.

A flash of anger ignited inside. "They were going to cut it down, can you believe it? So I saved it."

Jayden nodded, eyes still on Tommy. "I'm going to need my hand if I'm going to show you..." Her cheeks flushed and she looked away.

Tommy quickly released her hand and swallowed hard, trying to hide his own flaming reaction. "So, what did you want to show me?" he asked casually.

She nodded, turning all business. "Hand me your digipad." She pulled out her own and called up some information, then reached for Tommy's. She lifted a finger to her lips as she showed Tommy the difference in the two. Four crewmembers were unaccounted for.

Tommy frowned. Taking out his note pad he scribbled and passed it to her *Have we come in contact with any other vessels? Have any shuttles left the ship? Could they have used molecular transport to leave the ship?*

Her eyes grew wide as she watched him write out his questions. She pointed to the first and second, shaking her head *no*. For the third comment she bobbed her head from side to side, indicating it to be a possibility.

Tommy passed his hand over his mouth slowly, thinking. He took back the pad and scribbled another question. *Could you somehow find out about the transport records?*

She took the pad and pencil from his hands. Examining the pencil curiously, she held it in an awkward manner and began tracing lines on the pad. *Not without calling attention to myself, but I will try.* She handed the pad back to Tommy, obviously proud of her accomplishment.

Tommy took the note and tried to make out her writing. Her penmanship resembled the work of a kindergarten student. He'd never realized that these people didn't know how to write. He jot down another question and handed it back. *Do we have any information on these four people?*

Again, she shook her head, *no*. Lips pressed together, she focused a moment before writing.

He let out a sigh as he read the words. *We will know if and when they return.* That wasn't very reassuring, because if they did return, it would probably be to make a move. Tommy nodded. They'd have to be ready.

She took the pad back and printed another message. *You will have access to the SOB (souls on board) list during your medical rotation. Get into the habit of checking it daily, as though it was part of your duties. We cannot have random checks if we want to remain unnoticed.* She looked up at him momentarily and then added the last bit. *I just hope they don't come back between now and the start of your rotation.*

He considered her words, impressed by her reasoning and momentarily wondered if it had anything to do with her recent interest in Nancy Drew mysteries.

A week into Tommy's medical rotation he found himself accompanying Dr. Tounga during a colony transfer. This was the first time Tommy watched as a group had to be transferred from one continent to another, while remaining on the same planet. He had always believed it was easier for the people to adapt when remaining on their home planet, but as he shivered in the crisp morning air, he felt bad for the people coming from a tropical climate. He realized that these people would have never had to build well-insulated homes, or worry about heavy winter clothing. He figured it was like taking someone from South Beach Florida and relocating them to Tommy's home in the Canadian Rockies.

"Thomas!" Dr. Tounga called out. "I need you to help set up the clinic with Petra."

Tommy made his way to the shuttle and grabbed a storage bin filled with medical supplies. "Where do you want it?" he asked Petra as he followed her into the temporary building that had been erected overnight.

"Stack them here, along the wall." She pointed to the far end of the empty room. "They will be bringing in the furniture shortly."

Stacking the bin on top of the others, Tommy headed back out for another. He frowned when he saw more buildings being set up. "Is something wrong?" Dr. Tounga asked.

"I don't understand what's going on. I thought we were supposed to be discreet." He grabbed another bin and lifted it with a grunt. It was much heavier than the last.

"Here, allow me to help," Dr. Tounga said, grabbing his end of the bin. "In very few cases, the inhabitants are aware of us and of our role." He looked at Tommy and flashed a grin. "It makes things so much easier." He turned and entered the building backwards. "A cold spell is setting in. These people will have enough trouble adapting to their new environment without showing up half dressed in a snowstorm."

They deposited the bin none too gently and stretched their backs before heading back out. "Is winter on its way?" Tommy asked, concerned.

Shaking his head vigorously, Dr. Tounga moved around a cabinet that had just been unloaded from a shuttle. "No, and that's a good thing because these people are not used to temperatures below ten degrees Celsius."

Tommy gripped the edges of the cabinet and lifted. "Why aren't we using the anti-grav platforms to move all this?" He made his way slowly over the rough terrain, carefully taking steps to move the massive cabinet.

"They need them to move the wall sections." Tounga fumbled and had to steady his step. "Stop," he said sharply as he put his end down. He leaned his forehead on the cabinet, trying to catch his breath. After a moment he lifted his head. "I'll be right back." He turned on his heel and walked back towards the shuttle.

Tommy was relieved when he saw the doctor return with an anti-grav disk. Tommy reached for it and slid it under the cabinet. "Ready?" he asked Tounga. Visualizing the cabinet a foot off the ground the disk complied, leaving the men to guide the huge cabinet along.

"Where do you want it?" Tounga asked Petra.

"Finally," she exclaimed. "Set it down over here." She stuck her head into the adjacent room. "Ma'tys, you can start filling the cabinet."

Tommy watched as a young man appeared from around the corner. His white hair and ice blue eyes surprised Tommy, making him wonder if he was somehow related to Petra. "Dr. Tounga!" Ma'tys smiled enthusiastically at the sight of the doctor. He bowed slowly.

"This is Ma'tys," Petra explained. "He is the doctor we will be working with during the colony transfer."

"Nice to meet you," Tommy stammered. He'd thought they were the same age. A strange twinge hit Tommy in the pit of his stomach, and his breath caught audibly. He needed to get out of there.

Ice blue eyes held Tommy's, scanning, evaluating.

"Please excuse me a moment," Tommy said, hesitating only a fraction of a second before bolting out the door. Running on autopilot, he made his way past the mass of buildings, around the back of the Aurora and stopped dead.

Watoo sat on the ground, hugging his knees to his chest. "Go away."

Tommy dropped down beside him, resisting the urge to lay a hand on his shoulder. "You can't stay here, it's too cold." He blurted out the first thing that came to mind, but it was enough to get Watoo's attention.

"I can't do this…" his voice trailed off. He stared off into space, avoiding Tommy's gaze.

"What happened?" Tommy kept his voice low, controlled. He watched as his friend shuddered.

"I– I couldn't do it. There were too many people moving about…" He drew in a sharp breath and shuddered again.

It was unusual to have so many people working on a transfer, and Tommy figured Watoo was having flashbacks of the ambush. Considering he'd literally had his legs crushed and had come within an inch of his life, Tommy knew he had to get his friend away from the action. "Come on." He stood and helped Watoo to his feet. He moved cautiously, slowly guiding his friend around the shuttle. Once onboard, he sat Watoo down at the small table. "Where's your digipad?"

Watoo frowned but pulled the tablet from his pant pocket and laid it down on the table. Tommy pulled up the information on the transfer and skimmed through it quickly. The sound of footsteps had Tommy whirl around to face Eylann, Watoo's friend and immediate superior. She took in the scene in a critical fashion.

Tommy looked her right in the eyes and clenched his gut. "He is pushing himself a little too much for a first assignment." He tried to sound like the medical staff when imposing limitations. "I have managed to convince him to take a break, but he must not overdo it." He shot a glance at Watoo. "Or I am afraid you'll have to return to the ship." Continuing his act, Tommy stepped out of the shuttle, grabbed another crate of medical supplies and made his way back to where he'd left the others.

"Is everything all right?" Ma'tys asked, teeth chattering from the cold.

Tommy nodded, set the bin on the floor and removed his jacket. He handed it over to Ma'tys, who shook his head in refusal of the offering. "Trust me, I'm fine."

Hurrying to pull on the jacket, he shot Tommy a grateful look, before letting a look of sadness fill his eyes. "I don't know how we will ever adapt."

"How many of you are helping out today?" Tommy hadn't seen any others, but that didn't mean they weren't shivering out there somewhere.

"Only five." He held his arms tightly around his body.

Tommy took a moment to examine his clothing. It resembled light cotton, and there was no way it could keep him warm.

Jayden poked her head inside the medical building and smiled when she saw Tommy. "Have you seen Watoo?"

Tommy furrowed an eyebrow. "Yes, he's taking a break. I think he was trying to overdo it."

She looked over at Ma'tys and frowned when she noticed Tommy's jacket. "Are you cold?"

"Yes, nice of you to notice," Tommy said dryly.

She shot him a look he knew better not to challenge. "Be right back." She disappeared out the door, only to return less than a minute later with a survival jumpsuit and boots. "Here." She held out the bundle to Ma'tys who hesitated.

"Just pull it on over your clothing; the suit will adjust its size and temperature," Tommy said.

He quickly handed Tommy back his jacket, stepped out of his slippers and pulled on the jumpsuit. He looked around the room quickly before he sat down on the bin Tommy had brought in and shoved his feet into the boots.

"You have them on the wrong feet," Jayden said, amusement dancing across her features.

Tommy shot her a warning glance. "There are four others out there freezing somewhere. Do you think you could dress them as well?"

She nodded and turned to exit the room. "You sure Watoo's OK?"

Tommy shook his head just enough to let her know their friend was in trouble, then changed the subject. "Why wasn't there clothing provided for the colonists?"

"There was," she said bluntly. "But it was all sent to the colony."

Tommy rolled his eyes. "Great, now go find the others and dress them before they get frostbite."

She raised an eyebrow before disappearing out the door once again.

"Thank you so much," Ma'tys said sincerely.

"Ok, now let's see about turning the heat on in this thing." He looked around the room before stepping back outside to ask another crewmember for help.

"Haven't you ever seen one of these shelters before?" The stocky engineer asked.

"No, sir, this is my first time." Tommy watched as he stepped inside the soon to be medical building and moved to the side of the door.

"Rylan," the engineer identified himself. "Closing the door will help conserve heat." He laid his hand on the inner edge of the door frame and a door slid out from the wall, closing out daylight. Light streamed through the semi-transparent panels in the ceiling.

Ma'tys edged closer, eyes wide as he watched.

"The lights can be controlled here," Rylan explained. There were two thin metal strips beside the door, slightly darker in color at the bottom. "Slide you finger up the first one to control the lights." He moved his index up the strip and the room grew bright. "This one is for room temperature. You can feel the temperature as you slide your finger along the strip. Pick something comfortable, hold your finger on it a second and the room will adjust its temperature."

"Thank you!" Ma'tys said wholeheartedly.

Rylan left without another word and Tommy paused a moment to gather his thoughts. "Do you want me to help you set up in here or should I continue bringing in the bins?" Tommy asked.

"I will start placing my things," Ma'tys said. "You should return to check on your friend."

Tommy inhaled sharply, then nodded and hurried outside.

When he got to the shuttle Jayden was just stepping out its door. She held up a hand to prevent him from running inside. "He's fine. He's coordinating things from inside."

Tommy nodded. He knew if they both hovered over Watoo someone would notice. "OK, but keep an eye on him."

"I'll do my best," she said with forced exaggeration.

"Knock it off, Jayden. I'm worried about him." He passed his hand through his hair and took a few steps, thinking.

"I've got it," she reassured him. "Now you'd better get back to Tounga, before you realize his bedside manner is the nicest part of his personality."

Tommy wasn't sure how to take that until she laughed. "Just kidding." She whipped out her digipad. "You already have all assigned material, so maybe you should go help set up before someone notices you hanging around here…"

"Hey," Tommy said as she turned to leave, "I thought your rotation was supposed to be classroom prep."

She nodded. "It was, but since Watoo had just resumed his duties they figured it would be best if I helped him with all of his duties for a few days." She waved him off.

Tommy sprinted back to the medical center, and came face to face with Petra. "Where did you run off to this time?" She sounded like a grandmother scolding her grandson.

"I just wanted to make sure someone brought the others decent clothing," he spouted out an explanation.

"Hmm," she said, not believing him. "We need your help."

By the time Tommy made it back to his quarters he was wiped. He forced himself to take a quick shower and crawled into bed, exhausted. Sleep, however, was not forthcoming. He kept worrying about Watoo. He had been able to send his friend home earlier and had asked the CPU to not only keep an eye on Watoo, but to alert Tommy of any abnormal physical or emotional signs.

After tossing and turning for another half hour, Tommy made his way to the replicator for something warm to help him sleep. He almost dropped his mug when he turned and came face to face with his father. "I was reading in the common room," his father said. "I will not keep you as you are obviously very tired and in need of your sleep, but I would like to know how Watoo seemed to you."

Tommy forced himself to swallow his mouthful of warm liquid. "It was a bit much for him to start off with such a long day."

His father eyed him closely. "Did he seem fit for duty?"

"You know Father, I had so much to do…" Tommy tried to remain calm and tell the truth without giving away too much. "I did suggest he take a break at one point, but except for that time, I didn't see him again."

"Very well, but I expect you to keep me informed if you feel anything is off." His father turned to go back to his reading.

"Aren't you going to bed?" Tommy downed the contents of his cup and returned the empty mug to the replicator.

"Yes. I am almost done." His face softened. "You should go

and get some rest as well."

"I'm trying to." He forced a smile. He wanted to discuss Watoo with his father, but he didn't want his friend to get into trouble. Watoo probably needed a few days to adjust. "Good night, Father." He turned back towards his room to think about it.

By morning Tommy was exhausted. Today, he was off, so he didn't *have* to be anywhere by any specific time. He hadn't been obliged to remain to the end of the installation last night, but he'd wanted to see it through rather than show up in the morning and be told how it had gone. With a grunt he sat up, stretched and climbed out of bed. OK, so he'd obviously overdone it.

"Good morning, Thomas," his father greeted him as he emerged from his room. "Rough night?"

Tommy nodded, went to get a cup of coffee and dropped down on the couch next to his father. Sitting in silence, he focused on the sensation of the hot coffee sliding down with each swallow.

"Why did you remain behind after your shift was over?" His father's tone was curious, not challenging.

Leaning back against the couch Tommy sat the warm cup on his chest. "I wanted to make sure everything was set up and that everyone was settled."

"Would that be because you didn't trust the others to do their job or because you believed you could do it better?"

Tommy shot up so fast he spilt some of his coffee on himself. "Neither of them, Father!" He brushed the coffee from his top. "Why would you ask such a thing?"

His father passed a hand over his chin. "How do you think the others perceived your actions?" He shifted slightly, as he gave Tommy the 'once over'. "You are obviously tired. How would you be able to help today if there had been an emergency?"

Tommy was dumb struck. Feeling his cheeks flush, he was tempted to look away, but he held his ground. "I hadn't thought of that."

His father's eyes held his, searching deep within. His tone remained calm, calculated. "Every member of this crew has a job to do, and every job is important to the success of the mission. When someone is missing or unable to properly perform their duty, it has an impact on everything else."

Tommy thought about Watoo, and wondered if he should say anything. Then he wondered if he should mention the four mystery crewmembers, but having his father practically reprimand him for his error in judgment, especially since he thought he was doing a good thing, was enough. He didn't feel like falling any lower today. He let out a sigh.

"You are learning," his father continued. "This is why the length of specific training varies for each individual." He smiled apologetically. "I know you thought you were doing a good thing, and I am impressed by your determination and stamina, but you are a member of a team, and you must remember that." He stood, leaving Tommy alone to mull over his thoughts.

Tommy could hear him setting out breakfast, and though he was hungry, being around his father right now made him uncomfortable. Maybe this is what Jayden had been talking about, and Tommy wasn't even working directly with his father. He closed his eyes and let out a sigh.

"Let's eat," his father called from the dining area. "I was hoping to spend some time with you today. We have not had many opportunities to do so lately."

Tommy had mixed feelings. On one hand he agreed with his father, but on the other hand, his ego was still smarting. "Sure, what did you have in mind?" He made his way to the table and eyed the covered platter on the table. The strange smile on his father's face made him uneasy.

Watching as his father raised the cover from the platter; the unmistakable smell of French toast immediately set his mouth watering. "I thought you'd be pleased."

A grin spread across Tommy's face. He'd tasted so many really bad versions of French toast since he'd been here. He remembered the slimy green chunks his father had tried to feed him at one point. He had to agree that the taste was pretty darn close, but he couldn't get past the color and texture. "I'm almost afraid to taste it and ruin the illusion."

His father laughed. "Your idea about planting vegetables in the arboretum rather than simply storing seeds made me rethink some of our procedures. Two-Feathers gave us some chickens, and we have eggs now."

"Gracie," Tommy whispered.

His father shook his head as he served breakfast. "No, these are young chickens." He sat down and reached for the maple syrup. "Also from Two-Feathers. Our chef is quite thrilled."

Tommy smiled as he thought of Chei-Szu. He loved trying new recipes and especially loved having new ingredients to work with. "So what have you planned for us today?" he spooned a syrup covered mound into his mouth and almost moaned with pleasure.

"I thought we could do some endurance training, but since your energy level is so low, how about a game of pitch and catch?" He added more slices to his plate and poured himself juice. "Later on this afternoon I have to go down to the planet for my final assessment before we head out." He looked at Tommy. "You are welcome to join me."

He considered saying no, but he did want to get one last look around. He felt proud of all the work they'd accomplished, even if he had overstepped his boundaries. "OK, sounds great."

The morning activities had done wonders for Tommy. He felt comfortable around his father once again and had thoroughly enjoyed their time together. Now, as he walked beside his father on the planet he couldn't help but feel good about what he was doing. The nagging feeling about going back to Earth seemed almost like a dream, and Tommy knew if an intervention was needed, he'd be in a better position to help from the ship.

Ma'tys opened the door to the clinic, and stepped aside to let Tommy and his father in. Today, the young doctor wore several layers of clothing, and the building was a little too warm. "Commander, welcome back."

"Ma'tys," Dthau-Mahsz acknowledged. "You seem to have settled in quite nicely. Would you mind if we took a look around?"

The doctor bowed deeply. "Please, do come see." He stepped back and spread his arms as he launched into an explanation of the facility. Through the window Tommy caught site of Watoo. Something wasn't right. His friend moved across the yard nervously, looking over his shoulder and jumping occasionally.

The commander furrowed his brows and made contact through the link, asking if there was a problem.

"Excuse me, Doctor, Father, I'll be right back." Tommy hurried out of the room without another word and headed to where his friend seemed to have been going, but Watoo was nowhere to be seen. The crisp air bit through Tommy's clothes as he ran around the compound looking for Watoo. A ball of fear and panic hit Tommy, leading him on.

The new compound had buildings arranged around a circle that would likely become a park. Two extra rows of dwellings were arranged around the primary buildings, creating a labyrinth. Pausing a moment, Tommy focused on the emotion, letting it guide him straight to his friend.

At first, Tommy didn't see Watoo. It was the sound he'd made, like that of a wounded animal that guided his eyes to the form huddled on the ground behind a pile of storage bins. "There you are," Tommy said with relief. He took a step forward but froze when he saw the blood that covered Watoo's clothes and hands.

Watoo raised his head, a look of panic flashed in his eyes when he spotted Tommy and he cowered back against the bins. Tommy wasn't sure his friend even recognized him. Expanding the link to his father, he called for help and waited.

Gravel crunched underfoot as Tommy crouched down slowly. He needed to keep an eye on Watoo without scaring him off, at least until his father arrived. Tommy watched as Watoo wrapped his arms around his legs and tucked his head against his knees. His whole body was shaking, his breathing was irregular and there was a cut on the top of his head that continued to ooze blood.

Movement to the right of Watoo caught Tommy's eye. His father and Ma'tys, medical kit in hand, approached silently. "Easy, I'm not going to hurt you. It's me, Tommy." He moved closer, speaking softly to his friend as his father and Ma'tys eased in on each side, careful to keep out of Watoo's field of vision.

From the corner of his eye Tommy saw Ma'tys raise his hands, palms up, touch his forehead and then turn his palms toward Watoo who immediately began to relax before collapsing onto the ground. In a flash everyone was at Watoo's side. Ma'tys passed a hand over Watoo's bloodied form. Opening his medical pack Ma'tys pulled out two metal cylinders. "I'll do it," Tommy offered.

Ma'tys smiled awkwardly. "I have not had a chance to learn how they worked."

Pressing on an indentation, the two tubes lengthened into poles which Tommy proceeded to pull apart, revealing a shimmering film securely attached to the two metal lengths. Ma'tys had laid Watoo out on his back and given him a quick evaluation. Kneeling at his friend's head, Tommy crossed his friend's arm over his chest and prepared to lift him by the shoulders. In unison the doctor and commander positioned themselves on either side and lifted Watoo onto the stretcher, that now hovered an inch above the ground.

They walked in silence toward the medical building. Ma'tys laid a hand on Tommy's arm before he entered the room. "Not all of the blood on your friend is his," he said eyes widening.

Tommy looked at his father, not sure what to do. "You stay here with Watoo and assist Ma'tys as you can," his father said, stepping away from the stretcher.

"Yes, sir." A pang of guilt surfaced. Tommy wondered if he'd been honest with his father if Watoo might not have been injured.

A basin of warm water was thrust into Tommy's hands. "Clean his face and hands so we can see where the blood is coming from."

Tommy was sure Ma'tys already knew, but he laid the basin on a small cabinet near the head of the exam table. Wringing the warm water from the basin out of the cloth, he began to gingerly scrub the blood from his friends face. Tommy frowned when he saw a multitude of tiny cuts covering the left cheek and forehead. Had he run into a thorn bush of sorts?

"Here," Ma'tys said as he thrust a jar of salve into Tommy's hand without looking up. "Spread this over the wounds." His full attention remained on the gash on Watoo's head.

The commander entered the room with Eylann in tow. Her face still showed traces of blood from behind the cloth that covered her mouth and nose.

"Did Watoo do that to you?" Tommy blurted out.

She shook her head, barely raising her eyes to meet his. Tommy could already see dark circles forming under her eyes. Her nose was most likely broken.

Ma'tys laid a hand on Tommy's arm. "I have closed the wound. Finish cleaning him up, then make sure you apply the salve to the wound." He stepped around the table and made his way over to Eylann. He lifted her head and removed the cloth to examine her quickly before helping her to her feet and leading her into the next room.

As soon as the door closed behind the two, Tommy felt his father's presence. Not through the link, but towering over him. "You knew," his father said.

Tommy swallowed hard. "Father?"

Anger flashed in the commander's eyes. "You knew he was unfit for duty, yet you did not bother to report it."

Reaching for the salve, he shakily applied it to the cleaned wound. "I thought he was a little tired, and maybe nervous about returning to work." He replaced the lid on the jar and set it down on the cabinet. Lifting his head to face his father he wished he was anywhere but here. "I wasn't sure what to do," he said, feeling defeated.

"Thomas, there seems to be something bothering you. I am no more difficult to approach than before." His eyes searched Tommy's face. "We can openly discuss situations, about you and your peers. Had you mentioned a feeling of concern for Watoo I would have looked into it." He stepped aside to let two medical crewmen in.

"Commander," the tall, dark haired medical aide said as he awaited his orders.

"Accompany Watoo to medical bay. Transport directly there," the commander said. Turning to the medical cadet, he smiled. "Welcome, Pyper. You will accompany Eylann back to medical bay as well."

The sandy-haired girl stood stiffly in her cadet uniform. "Yes, sir!"

He raised a hand for her to stand down. "At ease. You and your parents will dine in my quarters tonight. We will have an opportunity to discuss ship's protocol." He motioned for her to enter the room behind him.

"Sir, thank you, sir." Without the slightest hint of emotion she stepped through the door and closed it behind her.

Tommy watched as the medical aide disappeared with Watoo's unconscious form. After a moment he turned to his father and frowned. "Did I know we were having company?"

"No, but only because you have been avoiding me." He paused a moment and stared off into space. "It is time to return to the ship."

The door opened and Ma'tys stepped back into the room. "Your crewmembers have returned to your vessel. I am sorry they were injured."

The commander waved off his comment. "An accident is an

accident. I want to thank you for your help with my crew."

Ma'tys smiled. "My pleasure, Commander." He inclined his head. "Thank you for all of this, and for everything that you have done for my people."

"Your stretcher will be returned short–" he was cut off by the reappearance of the metal cylinders. He pressed his lips together. "Before we leave, is there anything else you might need?"

"Summer," he said with an air of seriousness that solicited a laugh from the commander.

"We will be back shortly to check on you," the commander said, sobering. "In the meantime, you have a lot of work ahead of you."

"Again, thank you." Ma'tys took a step back and bowed deeply.

The room around Tommy was replaced with the raised platform in the molecular transport room. "Welcome back, Commander," the junior officer said. "All personnel present and accounted for."

"Thank you." He nodded and stepped down from the platform. "Come, Thomas."

Tommy sighed when he caught the 'uh-oh' look cross the senior officer's bronze face. He followed dutifully, one step behind his father. Half way to medical bay, and somewhere lost in his thoughts Tommy remembered the new medical cadet. "Who is Pyper?"

"She and her family have joined our crew. Her father is a security officer and a friend from long ago. He will replace Belek."

Belek, a name Tommy hadn't heard in almost three years. He

had been killed protecting his father from the Binari attack on Earth. "Do I know them?"

"No. You will meet them tonight." He stepped aside to let Tommy into medical bay.

"Commander, could I have a word with you," Mathezar called out from his office.

"I'll go check on Watoo, Father," Tommy said. He scanned the room to locate his friend. He was lying, unmoving, on a transparent exam table. Dr. Tounga looked up when Tommy crossed through the particle curtain.

"What happened to him?" Tounga was watching as the colored beams inside the table moved up and down along Watoo's body.

"I don't know. He was running from something, acting scared. I don't think he even recognized me when I went to him," Tommy offered. "Why is he still unconscious?"

"I'm not sure." He called up a holographic image of Watoo's body and leaned in close to examine it. "You say he was conscious when you found him?"

Tommy nodded. "Yes, Ma'tys did something to him that made him fall asleep."

"Ah." He made some adjustments to the controls at the foot of the exam table. "Stand back, please." A bubble of light engulfed Watoo's body and vanished just as quick. Watoo stirred, like a child waking from a fitful sleep.

Tommy let out a sigh of relief. He was beginning to worry. "What about his mental state."

Tounga shot Tommy an enquiring look. Crossing his arms across his chest he faced Tommy. "What have you noticed?"

Tommy drew in a long breath. "I saw him on the surface two days ago. He seemed nervous and uncomfortable with so many people around. I brought him inside one of the shuttles to take a break, but I had to return to my duties."

The doctor considered Tommy's words a moment. "So you are saying you thought him to be unfit for duty."

Tommy let out a sigh of defeat. "Yes, sir."

"Yet you did not report your observations," the commander said, stepping into the particle curtain.

"No, sir."

"I trust you will not repeat such an indiscretion. There were two crewmen injured, and that is two too many." His father took a step closer to Tommy and laid a hand on his shoulder.

"It won't happen again," Tommy answered with a hint of frustration in his voice. "But what will happen to Watoo now?" He tried to pull away from his father but his father turned him to face him.

"Explain."

Tommy threw his arms up into the air. "What's there to explain? He has PTSD or something!"

"You are probably correct in your diagnosis. I had read up on Earth illnesses and such when you first came onboard." Dr. Mathezar said from behind Tommy. "Now, he will receive the necessary care."

"Like what? Drug him so he doesn't feel or react anymore?" Tommy froze when he saw everyone's face drop at the same time.

Tounga let out a breath. "You will join me first thing tomorrow morning to assist in the recovery session." He gave a sympathetic smile. "We can help Watoo resume his life and his duties, by relieving him of the emotions linked to his trauma."

Tommy nodded.

"If you will excuse us, doctors, we are expected elsewhere." The commander motioned for Tommy to follow and the two left medical bay in silence.

"I'm sorry Father," Tommy said as they walked back to their quarters.

"I too have to remember that your background is different, and sometimes your reactions will also be different." His father pressed his lips together. "You will eventually be at ease here, but you will always carry knowledge and lessons from home, giving you a vast assortment of experiences and beliefs to weigh your decisions."

Tommy furrowed his brows. "What decisions?"

"In the future, you will have to make decisions...decisions that can mean the life or death for those who trust you." He stepped into their quarters. "Come now, we have to prepare for our four guests."

Tommy paused. "Four?"

"Yes, Pyper's family, why?" the commander eyed him strangely.

Tommy shrugged." I thought you guys only had one child per

family, if I look at the crew and their families."

The commander laughed and shook his head. "One day, my son. We will no longer be a mystery to you, and you will embrace your heritage."

"If I live that long," Tommy muttered to himself.

"Think about what you would like to eat, I am going to take a shower and change."

Tommy stood there alone, thinking. Actually, not thinking, because his mind went blank. He seemed to be having trouble keeping up. He grabbed something to drink and set himself down in the common room for a moment and wondered if the mystery four could be these same four people coming to dinner. He took a swallow of the chilled root tea. Well, he'd have to be creative with his dinner questions.

The door chimed just as Tommy finished laying out the last of the table settings. The only time they'd ever been more than four for dinner, since they often shared a meal with Jayden and Mathezar, was when Two-Feathers had visited. It had been a birthday surprise from his father.

His disappointment at seeing the two crewmen with their food was quickly dissipated when their guests appeared behind the dining staff. Tommy watched from the side as his father greeted the other man, a carbon copy of Belek, by firmly gripping him by the forearms before they briskly embraced one another. As Tommy observed the rare display, he noted the subtle differences between what he'd remembered of Belek and this man. Belek had been slightly shorter than the commander, and had a more muscular build. This man was as tall as Tommy's father, though not as buffed. Jet black hair and eyes adorned his mocha coloured skin, like his brother's, however his expression was not as harsh as he'd remembered Belek's to be...but then they'd been on a life and death mission at the time.

Tommy smiled awkwardly at Pyper as she stood stiffly beside her mother and little brother. The two men returned their attention to the room, smiling openly. "Kurok, this is my son Thomas," the commander said with pride.

Kurok held out a hand to the woman Tommy assumed was his wife. She was barely five feet tall, with the build of a gymnast, striking grey eyes and brown-and-gold streaked hair. Kurok smiled tenderly at her as she took her place at his side. "This is my wife, Sachi. My daughter, Pyper, already six months into her specific training, and this –" he said with a gesture that invited the boy, a more delicate version of himself, to join him, "is my son Joachim. He will be ten years old this coming week."

Tommy watched this man present his family with love and pride. He found it hard to believe he was Belek's brother, and wondered if Belek had left a family behind.

"Dinner is served, Commander," one of the crewman stated.

"Thank you," the commander acknowledged the black-clad dining staff. He turned his attention back to his guests "Shall we?"

"I am sorry to hear about Emma, Dthau-Mahsz. Mathezar had mentioned your loss." He paused as they seated themselves around the table.

Tommy watched a silent exchange pass between the two, and was surprised when his father discreetly closed his eyes and bowed his head.

"What's that?" Joachim exclaimed when the dining staff uncovered the platters.

Kurok shot his son a stifling glare and Tommy had to contain a smirk. There was a little more Belek in that regard. "Some of these come from my world," Tommy offered. Out of the corner of his eye he saw his father dismiss the dining staff, but he kept his attention on their young guest.

"But what if I don't like it?" he continued.

"Well, to know that you really don't like it, you have to taste it." Tommy was using one of his mother's tricks. "If you taste it, really taste it, and then decide you don't like it, you won't have to eat it." He watched the boy absorb the information. "Think about it. What if this turns out to be the best thing you've ever eaten? You might be passing up years of really great food." Tommy shrugged. "But then again, there'll be more for us if you don't try." He reached for a plate and passed it around, purposely ignoring the boy's reaction.

The commander winked at Joachim, and reached for the sweet potato ravioli, adding some to his plate. Everyone followed suit, openly ignoring the boy, yet Tommy caught an exchange of smiles between his parents when Joachim finally broke down and tasted the food. He was obviously a picky eater, but there was no doubt he'd enjoyed his supper.

After a pleasant meal, the group moved to the common room. Sachi excused herself, saying it was past Joachim's bedtime, and both men followed her to the door. Pyper sat across from Tommy, staring openly at him. After a few awkward minutes, he held her gaze back. "Is there something wrong?"

She stiffened a little more, something Tommy didn't think possible. "It's you…"

Tommy frowned. "What are you talking about?"

She shook her head and leaned forward. "You are the one our prophecy speaks of." Her voice was barely a whisper.

Both fathers returned from the dining area and Tommy watched as Pyper fell silent, morphing back to her reserved self. *Interesting*, Tommy thought.

Kurok seated himself beside his daughter while Dthau-Mahsz remained standing. Tommy could not read the expression on his father's face and the emotion coming from the link was like none he'd ever felt.

"Pyper, Thomas," the commander began to speak. "You are both here for a very specific reason. You are to witness an oath between myself and Kurok." He drew in a slow breath before continuing. "Our laws are very specific, and this is not a random act. My wife is no longer with me; therefore she cannot stand by me. This means, Pyper, that your mother cannot stand by your father."

"Does this have any impact on us," Pyper asked, an undertone of uncertainty in her voice.

"No, although you will know if ever the bond is broken," Kurok answered gravely.

"You mean if one of you dies..." Tommy offered.

"Yes," his father answered. "You must understand that although you are both technically old enough to stand witness to such a pact, you would however, be the youngest to actually do so."

"Should you choose to stand down, then we will be permitted to do this on our own," Kurok said. Tommy couldn't tell by his tone whether he was for or against them being part of it. When he tried to get an impression through the link, he found neutral feelings there as well. Almost as though he sensed what Tommy was thinking, Kurok added, "The decision must come from within each of you. If only one of you is in favour of being part of this, then we will proceed alone."

"Take a few minutes to think about it," the commander said.

Tommy shifted uncomfortably in his seat. He wasn't sure how he felt about this, probably because he didn't really understand the ritual, nor what was expected of him. Who was he kidding; he knew absolutely nothing about it.

"Feel free to ask any questions," the commander added.

"Why are you doing this?" Tommy asked. He remembered Belek had taken this oath with his father, and that he had lost his life because of it.

The commander sat beside Tommy and opened the link as he held his son's gaze. "Just as there are people in your society who receive added protection, not only for themselves, but their family, the same is expected for me."

Tommy recoiled. "Like a movie star or something?" He didn't understand, or maybe he didn't want to.

Pyper flinched. "You mock your father! Don't you know who he is?"

The commander held up a hand. "No, he does not."

"But this was always to be your destiny!" Pyper exclaimed, rising to her feet.

"Sit down," Kurok said calmly to his daughter. "This was also to be Belek's destiny, and yet he is no longer here to fulfill that role. You know because of the link, the information has not been shared yet, and you are expected to remain silent."

Tommy raised both hands to make them stop. None of this made any sense. "What are you, some kind of king?"

His father held his son's gaze, and slowly opened the link. Tommy's breath caught as he absorbed a lifetime of information, beliefs and traditions. How could he have not known? How could his father keep this from him? Tears streamed down his face as he finally began to understand the role of his father's, no, of *his* people in this galaxy.

I'm sorry, Father. Why didn't you show me this before, why didn't you explain? Tommy asked through the link.

"I had hoped you would have come to this realization on your own, that you would have embraced your people and your heritage." He laid a hand on Tommy's shoulder. "I am not asking you to turn away from your mother's world and all it has given you."

Tommy nodded, swallowing the lump that had formed in his throat. "What do we have to do?" He wiped the tears from his face and drew in a breath of determination.

Kurok looked at his daughter. "What is your decision?"

She lowered her eyes. "I will stand by you, Father, always."

The commander nodded. "So be it." He looked at his son. "Are you ready?"

Tommy's chest expanded with pride. "I will be honored to stand by you, Father." He bowed slightly, barely able to control the shaking he felt within.

Satisfied, his father nodded. "We shall begin."

Clearing a space for the group to sit on the floor of the living room, the commander and Kurok knelt facing one another. A small stone box was placed on the floor between the men. Tommy recognized the stone; the pendant he'd worn on Earth had been made from it. Closing their eyes, they leaned in close enough for their foreheads to touch. Tommy felt a rush of energy, of knowledge, and waited for his cue to act.

The two men extended their arms out to each side, their fingers laced together. Tommy and Pyper moved in unison, kneeling with their foreheads touching the extended fingers. For a brief instance, all four souls were connected. All hearts beat as one. Life force energy rose up and flowed through the two men, brushing the souls of the witnesses present.

No words were spoken, no sounds made, just the solemn promise of a life for a life. Time stood still. A burst of colored light filled the room and floated down around them like feathers drifting on a breeze. A vibration grew into a single note, then a chord, until they were caressed by music that lifted their souls and bound them with a delicate silver thread.

A moment of total truth, of comprehension came upon them. Acceptance and love filled them. Drawing a breath in unison, they sat back on their heels and began to breathe separately, until they were able to focus and move again.

Opening the cylindrical stone box, the commander removed a translucent stone on a thread of light and handed it to Kurok. Once around his neck, it vanished.

Taking a second stone form the box, the commander slipped it over his head and Tommy watched as it too, vanished. Moving instinctively, Tommy placed his palm over the stone. He felt the heat it generated and heard the song it sang.

No one spoke again. When it was over, the room was restored and Kurok left with his daughter. Tommy turned and stared at his father a moment, but there was nothing to say, not even a 'good night'. In contented silence, they each headed to their rooms. Tommy dropped down onto his bed, his head swirling with images and information. He tried to remember all he had seen, all the information he had absorbed, but it was fading fast. What was crystal clear minutes ago, was morphing into a fleeting memory. Fatigue settled heavily on him, and before he had the chance to sort through any of the memories, sleep claimed him.

Chapter 7

By the time his father emerged from his room the next morning, Tommy had been waiting at the table for over an hour. He had questions, many questions, and he needed answers.

"I thought you would have at least had coffee waiting," his father said with a smile when he saw Tommy at the table. He paused and surveyed his son with a more critical eye. "Set out breakfast, I'll be with you in a minute."

Tommy nodded, pushed his chair back and headed to the replicator. He called up a plate of fresh fruit slices, a pan of 'sticky loaf', which resembled a type of honey-glazed oatmeal bread with nuts, and two mugs of coffee. As he was going to sit back down, he spotted his note book on the table by the entrance and went to get it. He'd sketch while he waited for his father.

Memories came back as he flipped through the pages of the old note book, and he couldn't help but smile. Stuff about Mom, his friends, doodles at the bottom of assignment notes, plans and projects he'd had for his future. He passed his hand over a note left by Mom. "Miss you, Mom," he whispered. Flipping the page, he smiled at the awkward scribbling of Jayden's words.

He inhaled sharply, —*he was in medical bay, turning away from Tounga to carry out an order when he came face to face with a smiling Jayden. Warmth spread through his insides as he returned the smile. "What are you doing here?" he asked.*

"Watoo is resting, so I have been reassigned here for the week." She bobbed on the tips of her toes. "What do you need?"

"Is everything all right?" his father asked, drawing Tommy instantly back to their quarters.

Tommy jumped. "You startled me," he blurted.

His father nodded, eyebrows raised. "So I noticed." He eyed Tommy's notepad. "Anything interesting?"

Dropping his gaze to the book in his hands he shook his head and closed it. "No, just a bit of nonsense." He placed the book on the chair at his right and drew in a deep breath as he frantically struggled for composure.

Taking a seat across from Tommy, the commander's gaze never left his son. "You appeared to have been far away."

"About as far as medical bay." He reached for a piece of sticky loaf, his eyes meeting with his father's fleetingly. He waved off the comment. "Just thinking about stuff I have to do later on."

His father nodded, seemingly accepting of the explanation. "I am assuming, since you have been sitting at the table since 0445, that you have questions."

Tommy paused in mid chew and swallowed abruptly. "You knew I was up and you left me sitting here with my questions?" He chased the lump of food down with a gulp of coffee.

"I was asleep," he said in an offended tone. "You were bombarding me with your thoughts, and kept interrupting my integration."

"Integration of what?"

The commander deposited his fork on the edge of his plate. He began to speak but stopped, and his face softened. Pressing his lips together he drew in a breath. "I forget that you are still missing details and information."

Tommy exhaled sharply. "There are days when I wonder where my place is. I am no longer at home on Earth, and there are times when I most certainly don't fit in here."

"You are too hard on yourself, Thomas. You might have been home with your mother, feeling the same way." His father helped himself to some of fruit and passed the serving dish to Tommy.

"What happened last night? What does all this mean? Who or what are you?" Well, not the most tactful approach, but he'd said it.

His father swallowed a sip of coffee and put his cup back down on the table. "The transfer of information was complete. You should have all the answers to your questions."

"Dad, come on." Tommy didn't hide the frustration in his voice. "What are you, some kind of sovereign, president or leader? What exactly happened last night? What is expected of me or of Kurok in all this?"

His father passed a hand over his mouth. "You were witness to the oath between Kurok and myself."

"Which means he is sworn to protect you with his life, right?"

His father nodded.

"Are you sworn to protect his life with your own?"

His father pulled back and grimaced. "No, of course not, not in the same way, but that does not mean I will not do everything in my power to protect him."

"What exactly does 'not in the same way' mean?" He pushed his plate away, no longer in the mood for food.

"Thomas, why is this so hard for you to accept? You have this kind of practice on Earth as well." Finishing the last bite he rose and collected the plates, returning them to the replicator.

"Well yeah, for government figures, royalty, the pope, singers, movie stars and criminals…." He paused at how ridiculous the group sounded. "Where does that put you?" He couldn't imagine his father in any of those roles…could he?

"The official announcement will not be made for some time, years even," his father explained, choosing his words carefully, "but I will eventually be called to lead our people."

"Are you related to the Sovereign?" Tommy was trying desperately to grasp the concept.

His father frowned, shaking his head as he stood. He motioned for Tommy to move to the common room, and tugged on his uniform top before sitting back down on their brown sofa. "Have you forgotten your history lessons so soon?"

Tommy racked his brain, searching for that part of his lessons. For some reason he could not remember anything about the governing of these people. "Father, I don't remember and I can't seem to think straight. There was too much information to absorb last night and I think I missed something."

His father leaned forward and looked Tommy in the eyes. "Sovereignty is not obtained through blood lines the way it is on your planet. Nor is it from any form of dictatorship, or the expressed choice of the people through voting. The selection is based upon an endless number of factors, abilities and performance. I would suggest you read up on it."

Tommy tilted his head. "So you are going to be king."

"Sovereign."

He passed a hand through his hair and stood, agitated. He paced around the back of the room, stopping to look out the port hole at the passing stars. "Does everyone already know about you being sovereign?"

"No, and it is not to be discussed with anyone." His tone was firm, final.

Tommy turned away from the stars and sat on the ledge of the port hole. "But what about what we did last night, don't they know? What was Pyper referring to? "

"About me being next in line as Sovereign? No. They expect me to lead the crisis intervention program."

"Well then how can you explain doing what we did?" Tommy threw his arms up. "We had this whole ritual thing going on…" his voice trailed off.

"As commander of a crisis intervention vessel I am to have one *verndari*," he said as though that explained everything.

Tommy stared at him. "Verndari?"

"It means protector, of sorts." He paused for a moment and looked off into space as though he was consulting something, someone. "Shouldn't you get ready for your shift in medical bay?"

With a frown Tommy waved him off. "I still have time. So, when you say protector you mean body guard?"

"Yes."

"But Belek has been dead for three years, why wait so long?" So much about the unknowns and subtleties of this culture frustrated Tommy. "And if I got the impression through the link or ritual that you were to be some kind of important person, don't you think they'll know about it too?"

His father smiled and gestured for Tommy to come back to the couch. "There has been a verndari team close by, which is probably why the attack on me failed. The difference here is that they are not sworn solely to me."

"OK, so they're just like body guards."

With a half nod he continued. "Close enough. Their primary duty is to me, secondary to the ship. As for Kurok and Pyper, they did not see or feel what you did. Likewise, you did not see or experience the totality of the link between Kurok and myself. Deep down he knows of both his and my destiny, so it will come as no surprise when it is announced, but for now, he will overlook the information."

Tommy pressed his lips together. "But you do know that things tend to get around on the ship, right?"

"Such as you and Jayden searching for the mysterious four?" A smile spread across his lips, reaching his eyes.

"OK, we were worried about you." He slapped his hands to his thighs and stood. "Now I'm going to get ready." He took a few steps and then paused. He let out a sigh and turned to face his father. "You could have said something."

An eyebrow rose slightly. "And you should have."

Tommy considered his words. He was right. Having said something would have saved them all a lot of worry and discomfort. "Was it Kurok and his family?"

"No."

He clenched his jaw. "But you knew about it?"

"Yes."

"And you're not going to tell me who they were." He stared at his father, watching a hint of amusement play on his features.

"No. Not yet." He rose to his feet. "I must also prepare for my day."

Once in medical bay, Tommy was able to push his thoughts away and focus on his tasks. For now, he was something of a medical aide and he enjoyed helping out. "Thomas," Tounga called out from his office. "I would like to see you a moment."

Tommy handed the sample to the technician and headed for Tounga's office. He poked his head into the doorway, not sure if this would take long.

Waving him in, Tounga lit up the table top with a schedule

display. "Since I only have you to mentor, I will offer you two choices. You can maintain a cadet schedule, basically working and studying during the day, or you can match your schedule to mine." He pointed to the table top. "Here, you would be on evenings and once every rotation we would be on nights." He looked to see if Tommy was following.

Taking a moment to consider his options, he decided to embrace the experience. "Why not. I think I would like to follow you."

"Very well. The schedule will be sent to your digipad." He punched in the command. "This afternoon you have a three hour study period, and then you will return for the last hour." He settled back in his chair, arms crossed, and studied Tommy. "How do you feel about your rotation so far?"

Tommy paused a moment to go over his brief experience as a med cadet. He had helped out a bit over the years, but his role was much more active now. "I like the teamwork, and I enjoy helping out very much. I still have trouble dealing with the sight of blood and suffering, especially when I feel helpless to do anything about it." He shrugged. "I'm not sure I am cut out for this department, but I look forward to my time here."

Tounga smiled. "Your reaction is normal, and quite healthy. A good healer can empathize with his patient. If you were already detached from their condition I would have to question you being here." He stood with a satisfactory nod. "Shall we carry on?"

He stepped out of the office and turned away from Tounga to continue working, when he came face to face with a smiling

Jayden. Warmth spread through his insides as he returned the smile. "What are you doing here?" he asked.

"Watoo is resting, so I have been reassigned here for the week." She bobbed on the tips of her toes. "What do you need?"

A spark of déjà-vu came over him, leaving him momentarily dizzy. He brought a hand up to his head and stumbled back a step.

"Are you OK?" Jayden grabbed hold of his arm to steady him.

Quickly regaining his composure, he smiled down reassuringly at her. "Yeah, I haven't had lunch yet."

"OK, then lunch it is." She turned away, tugging on his sleeve for him to follow.

"Just give me a minute to inform Dr. Tounga."

"Go on," Dr. Mathezar said from behind Tommy. "I will let him know. I have to discuss something with him anyway."

"Thank you," Tommy said as Jayden increased her speed towards the door, still holding tight to his sleeve. "Stop pulling, please. I'm coming."

The cadet lounge was all but empty, save for two girls sitting in the far corner of the room, talking animatedly. There was one from a botany rotation, the other from geology. They had half-empty plates on the table nestled between the stuffed bistro-type armchairs.

They didn't even look up when Tommy and Jayden entered. "What do you feel like eating?" Jayden asked, hovering by the replicator.

He shrugged. "You pick. Anything would be good at this

point."

She nodded and turned back to the panel on the wall. Punching in her selection, the door lifted and she withdrew a long rectangular platter filled with bite-size pieces. Smiling, she set it down between them. "Here, instant buffet."

He laughed and reached for a piece, popping the warm bite into his mouth. "Not bad," he said still chewing.

"So, what happened back there?" She licked a crumb from her finger and reached for another morsel. "And don't bother lying this time."

Sobering a little, he passed his hand through his hair and let out a breath. "I'm not really sure," he said honestly. He searched her face. "Have you ever had déjà-vu?"

Her eyes widened. "Maybe if I knew what that was…"

Tommy pursed his lips. "Well, it's like something happens, and you get the impression that it has happened before." He grimaced. There had to be a better way to explain it. "Only it's more than that. It's like living it over again."

She shook her head. "Not to me, but I've heard of it happening to others." She looked over her shoulder to where the other girls still sat. "Did it happen to you?" she whispered.

He exhaled slowly. "I'm not sure." He passed his hand over his face. "Look, let's just drop this."

Jayden picked up another bite, nibbled at the edge and then popped it in her mouth. She wiped her fingers on her pants. "OK, but just this time. Promise me you'll tell me if it happens again."

He nodded.

She leaned in closer and laid a hand on his knee. "Now, tell me what went on in your quarters last night."

He pulled back, startled, and he wasn't sure if it was because of the touch or the question. Tounga walked into the lounge and headed straight for them, not giving him the chance to answer. Standing, Tommy brushed a crumb from his uniform top. "Dr. Tounga, is something wrong?"

The doctor shook his head. "No, I knew you had your study period coming up and I wondered if you could postpone it until later on today. There is a procedure I would like you to observe." He offered a nod of greeting in Jayden's direction.

"Sure," Tommy said, not knowing what he was getting in to, but he had to get away from Jayden's questioning. "Now?"

Tounga nodded. "Now." He turned on his heel and headed for the door.

Tommy shot a glance towards Jayden. "I'll see you later," he mouthed as he hurried after the doctor.

By the time Tommy entered his quarters, he had only one thing in mind, food. He'd shower later, because right now he needed to eat. The enticing aroma of his mother's vegetable stew greeted him when the doors slid open, and Tommy's stomach growled in response.

"I have only been home for twenty minutes myself," his father said. He set the steaming pot of stew on the table. "The CPU informed me of your change in schedule, so I figured you'd be hungry." He sat down at the table.

"Starving," Tommy admitted. "Just give me a minute to wash up."

Half the meal was gone before either of them said a word. "Tounga informed me that you had observed the implant of the learning chip as well as the tracking chip," his father said casually. "What did you think about that?"

A chill ran up Tommy's spine. The image of the tiny chip being inserted at the base of the child's skull came to mind. He'd watched it blend into the tissue of the exposed epidural layer around the spinal cord, making it all but impossible to remove. Someone else might have thought it to be fascinating, but Tommy found it upsetting. "I still panic at the thought of such a practice, though I accept the reasons behind it. It was much more complicated than I had expected." He shuddered. "I can't believe Mathezar did it to me right here on the couch."

His father nodded. "He is very skilled."

"Remember my comment about things getting around?"

Turning all his attention to Tommy, the commander waited for the explanation.

"Well, Jayden asked me what went on in our quarters last night." He was sure his father's face grew a shade darker.

"What did you tell her?" His tone was a little sharper than necessary.

"Nothing, Father. Tounga showed up at just that moment." He took a mouthful of stew. If he closed his eyes he could imagine being back on the farm with his mother.

"And?" His father put his fork down and waited.

He swallowed. "And nothing. I ran out after Dr. Tounga."

"Hmm, so she will most likely pursue the topic."

Tommy snorted. "That's an understatement. It's like wondering if a dog will pick up a bone." He sobered. "What do I tell her?"

"The truth," his father said, finishing his last bite.

Tommy did a double take. "But you told me not to say anything to anyone."

"Not all of it. Just tell her that Belek's brother, and family, had dinner with us. We shared stories and reminisced." He stood to clear the dishes. Two pieces of chocolate cake were brought to the table.

Accepting the treat with a grateful smile, Tommy said, "Had I known I'd get such great food for being late, I would have done so more often."

His father laughed under his breath. "I was feeling somewhat nostalgic, and missing your mother tonight."

The admission caught Tommy by surprise. "I didn't think you still thought of her," he said in a hushed voice.

His father stiffened. "She was part of my soul, a part that can never be replaced." He touched his hand to his chest. "She still lives here, and every day, I hear her words, her laughter."

Tommy felt the sting of tears behind his eyes. "Then why do I have a hard time clearly remembering her face…I have to look at pictures to remember." His voice sounded bitter.

His father steepled his fingers and then brought them to his lips. "You are relying on your memory, your head." He tapped a finger to his temple. "Open the link. No, not to me, to your mother."

Tommy shook his head. "But I don't have a link to Mom."

His father nodded. "Close your eyes. Come on, trust me." His voice softened. "It is there, it has always been there."

Tommy settled back in his chair, drew in a deep breath, and closed his eyes. He let the link to his father expand, and he felt his father guide it. Like a blind person being led down an unknown path, Tommy clung to his father's presence. She was there, smiling at him. He could see her, smell her faint citrus scent, and when he reached out to touch her he was sure he could feel her.

His father drew back and left Tommy to his memories.

A touch on Tommy's shoulder drew him out of his memory, and back to the dining room table with his father. "Just remember," his father said, "the past is behind you, and though you may visit often, you live in the present. Do not use it as an escape."

Tommy nodded. "Thank you, Father."

"It is time to get some rest. Tomorrow, since we are both on the afternoon shift, I have reserved an endurance training room for mid-morning."

A smile spread across Tommy's face. "I could use a good

workout."

"Then it is settled, I will see you in the morning." He stood and waited for Tommy to follow.

Tommy rose to his feet and hugged his father on impulse, grateful the hug was returned. "Good night, father." He made his way to his room, settled under his covers and opened the link to his past, letting it come alive and surround him.

The CPU broke through Tommy's thoughts and memories. "Your father left to meet with engineering. He will meet you for endurance training as planned," the flat voice said.

Sitting up with a start, Tommy rubbed his eyes. He'd only been in bed a few minutes, it couldn't be morning already. "How much time do I have?"

"Forty-five minutes before the start of your session."

He tossed his covers aside and hurried to the shower. Twenty minutes later, dressed and downing a glass of farou tonic, he made his way to the endurance training center. No sense eating before the workout. He still couldn't believe he'd been awake all night reliving memories. Now he understood his father warning about not living in the past. This was nothing like calling up a memory; you could actually relive the moment, even though it was not real.

The effects of the farou tonic kicked in, sharpening his senses, but the underlying fatigue remained. Rounding the corner to the training room, he stiffened as a familiar tingle in the bottom of his gut appeared… –*as he walked into medical bay for his afternoon shift, he heard Jayden arguing with Watoo. Making his way behind the particle curtain, he was surprised to see her trying to calm Watoo as he struggled to sit up. "What's going on?" he blurted out. They both froze.*

Jayden stepped back, and pointed to Watoo. "We had to restrain him, he won't cooperate."

Tommy let out a breath and passed his hands through his hair. "Give me a minute," he said to Jayden.

Her mouth opened in protest, but she shut it, stiffened and walked away.

"What's going on?" he asked Watoo.

"She wanted to touch me," he said with a hint of exasperation.

Tommy laughed, surprised by the comment. "Would you like me to tend to you?"

Watoo lay back in submission. "Fine."

"Did she restrain you?" he asked. Turning away so Watoo couldn't see the look of amusement on his face, he released the field.

"Good, you're here," his father pulled him from the vision.

Tommy shuddered as he forced himself to focus on his father.

Concern filled the commander's eyes. "Is everything all right?"

Tommy nodded, looked up at his father and forced a smile. "Just lost in thought."

"You missed breakfast this morning; did you eat anything before coming here?" His gaze scanned Tommy from head to toe.

He let out a breath. "I drank something before coming," he answered honestly. "I didn't want to do this on a full stomach."

Eyes still on Tommy, his father shifted and crossed his arms. "Would you prefer if we rescheduled?"

"No, I'm good," he said reassuringly.

The door to the training room opened and they stepped inside. As they put on their harnesses and made their way up the ladder to the platform, Tommy could feel his father studying his every move.

"If your reflexes are down, this could be dangerous," his father commented.

"I'm fine, really." He didn't need the added pressure of his father's scrutiny.

"What time did you get to sleep last night?" his father asked, fastening the safety cable to their belts.

Tommy exhaled sharply. "I didn't, because I got lost in my memories." He looked at his father. "I didn't know it would do that."

Looking back over his shoulder his father smiled and shook his head. Without making a comment, he grabbed hold of the handles on the zip line and leapt from the platform.

Grateful to have not been reprimanded, Tommy positioned himself on the landing and gripped the handles firmly. He drew in a determined breath and launched himself through the first set of obstacles in the holographic forest. Tree-top adventure centers had become popular on Earth, but this version took it to a whole new level of challenges and excitement. Tommy loved the ever-changing sequence of obstacles.

Stepping out of the shower after an exhilarating workout, Tommy had just enough time to eat before the start of his shift. He pulled out his digipad and looked over the information that had been added since his last shift, and saw that Dr. Tounga had already defined his workload for the day. He would have to apply what he had learned in study period yesterday, because today was going to start with Tommy conducting routine physicals on three crewmen. There was one period entitled "Tounga" that sparked his curiosity. He'd know soon enough what the day held in store for him.

As he walked into medical bay, his attention was drawn to the sounds of Jayden arguing with Watoo. Making his way behind the particle curtain he already knew what he'd see, Jayden trying to calm Watoo as he struggled to sit up. "What's going on?" They both froze.

Jayden stepped back and pointed to Watoo. "We had to restrain him, he won't cooperate."

Tommy let out a breath and passed his hands through his hair. "Give me a minute," he said to Jayden. He couldn't shake the strange sense of déjà-vu that took over again.

Her mouth opened in protest, but she shut it, stiffened and walked away.

"What's going on?" he asked Watoo.

"She wanted to touch me," he said with a hint of exasperation.

Tommy stifled his laugh. "Would you like me to tend to you?"

Watoo lay back in submission. "Fine."

"Did she restrain you?" he asked innocently, turning away so Watoo couldn't see the expression on his face, and released the field. Moving to the foot of Watoo's bed Tommy called up the information on the treatment he was to receive. He could see no reason why Watoo would resist. "Why didn't you let Jayden tend to you?"

He stared up at the ceiling. "I just want to be left alone."

Tommy moved to Watoo's side and placed a hand on his friend's shoulder. "I cannot leave you alone. I'm here to help, and that's what I intend to do." He paused, hoping for a reaction, but Watoo continued to avoid his gaze. "Your options at this point are this; either you receive help from me or from Jayden." He had an idea, but he was going to have to talk to either Dr. Tounga or Dr. Mathezar about it. "I'll give you a few minutes to think about it." He stepped out of the particle curtain and went off to find one of the doctors.

"Thomas," Mathezar called to him from his office.

Petra nodded as Tommy stepped past her and entered the office. "Yes?"

"You will tend to your duties without Dr. Tounga while he is in surgery," he began. "I will see to Watoo's needs myself, since the idea of being treated by a student increases his stress."

Tommy nodded enthusiastically. "Yes, Sir. I wanted to talk to you about that as well."

The doctor put down the digipad he had been studying and motioned for him to sit. "I'm listening."

Tommy clasped his hands together on the desk and leaned forward. "I think Watoo is suffering from post-traumatic stress disorder, and back home there's a technique that is used to stimulate left-brain, right-brain in such a way that the emotional response is detached from the memory of the event."

The doctor stared at him as though he had been speaking a foreign language. "I dare say I cannot imagine how that would work."

Tommy's heart sank. He really wanted to find a way to help his friend.

"Do you have any data on this procedure?" Mathezar asked.

"Really?" A surge of hope filled him. He leaned in closer to the doctor. "On Earth it's called EMDR, for eye movement desensitization and re-something…" he made a face. He couldn't remember the last word.

The doctor's table top lit up and he began tapping and sliding things around, calling up all sorts of information. He pushed the information across the table and turned it towards Tommy. "Is this it?"

Reading quickly through the information, Tommy nodded. "This one uses sound, but I think it's pretty much the same."

Mathezar nodded. "I am going to take some time to study this treatment. If it seems appropriate, then we can give it a try. Finish your rounds and take your meal break afterwards."

Tommy nodded and stood. "I really hope this works," he said sincerely.

"Yes, as do we all."

A glimmer of hope filled Tommy as he set off to finish his work.

Two hours later, he made his way from medical bay to the lounge for end-of-day meal. A familiar tingle crept up on him as he turned down the last corridor. Jayden stood outside the door, waiting for him. Her cheeks flushed slightly and she looked away when their eyes met.

Warmth spread through his chest at the sight of her and his smile grew. "Hi," he said. "I think we have a solution for Watoo."

She reached for his hand and gave it a squeeze. "That's a relief."

Heat spread through his hand like fire, and he returned the squeeze, but released it suddenly when the cadet lounge door opened. He cleared his throat. "Have you eaten yet?"

She shook her head. "No, I was waiting for you." She stepped into the room, twisting her hands together. "Do you want to share the same thing as last time?"

"Yeah, sure. I don't have all that much time." He went to get some beverages before he settled into a corner seat. He wanted to get back to Watoo

She set the tray down between them and took a seat. "I added a few extras," she said, stuffing a small morsel into her mouth.

They ate in a comfortable silence for a few minutes, each of them lost in their own thoughts. Tommy focused on the treatment planned for Watoo, hoping there would be some relief for his friend. It hurt to see him like this, to watch him suffer helplessly.

"Are you going to answer?" Jayden laid a hand on his arm, lightly. She withdrew it quickly when Tommy focused on her.

"I'm sorry," he said with a crooked grin. "I have a lot on my mind. What was it that you said?"

She shook her head. "That's twice now. I'm going to start thinking you don't want to be with me…" her voice trailed off.

He reached out and touched her cheek with the back of his fingers. "Not going to happen."

Her eyes widened, and she swallowed hard. "Um, I asked you if you had any more of those flashes you'd mentioned the other day."

He stiffened visibly, giving himself away.

"What? What is it?" Her face was filled with concern.

He blinked, trying to regain control. "It's nothing, really. I think my mind is playing tricks on me…trying to come up with a solution for Watoo." He shook his head. "I've been under a lot of stress lately, you know, with that whole Fardoc thing, then my father getting poisoned. I think it's been a little crazy lately, that's all."

She eyed him as she chewed on her lower lip. "Well, what do you see? Is it like a dream?"

He passed a hand through his hair and settled back in his seat.

"No, it's like..."

"Is it like a memory?"

He reached for another bite and focused on the flaky morsel as he ate it. Brushing the crumbs off his hands he leaned in closer. "No, it's more like the images we get through the link."

She pulled back sharply and tears filled her eyes.

"What's the matter? What'd I say?" He reached out and took both of her hands in his. They were so tiny compared to his.

She tried to force a smile but the corners of her mouth twisted downward. She pulled her hands back and wiped away at the tears. "It's just that I don't really get images anymore, not since Mother died."

"I'm sorry, Jayden, I don't know what to say." He pressed his lips together as he watched her, longed to hold her. The last thought caught him off guard, causing him to jump awkwardly to his feet. Uncomfortable now, he collected the dishes and returned them to the wall slots. "We should head back," he said gently.

Jayden nodded and stood, following a step behind.

Tommy paused in the corridor and turned back to her. "Come on, catch up or people will start to wonder if we had a fight."

She sighed and moved forward.

"Remember the other day when we were talking about our rotations?" He tried to make small talk.

She shrugged. "What about it?"

"Well, you seemed surprised by my rotation schedule, but you never said why." He deliberately walked past medical bay doors and continued along the corridor.

"Because you have almost every department," she exclaimed.

He paused, confused. "But I thought we all had the same schedule."

She shifted her weight onto one leg and placed a hand on her hip. "Specific training, to prepare us for our future, remember?" Her eyes widened as she leaned in to him.

"We both got crisis intervention vessel, so what you're saying doesn't make sense." He turned and continued walking.

"You don't get it, do you?" She caught up to him and pulled him to a stop. "In my case, the fact that I have both medical and botanical rotations is already rare. The majority of people have only one field of study, yet you seem to have rotations through every department."

"I still don't get it."

She held him by the arm. "Well you better be catching on a whole lot faster in the future, because I think I'm looking at the next crisis intervention commander." Her eyes searched his.

"You're serious…" his voice trailed off in disbelief.

"How can you not know? Your father must have said something about it."

He passed a hand through his hair and walked a small circle around Jayden. He tried to remember being told he'd lead a crisis intervention crew. He'd assumed he'd be part of the crew. "No, not that I can remember, and I don't think it's something I'd forget.

"Come on," she said pulling him back towards medical bay.

"We're going to be late."

Tommy waited impatiently outside the room while they treated Watoo. From where he paced, not even a sound could be heard and Tommy was beginning to wonder if they really were inside. "Shouldn't you be studying by now?" Petra asked as she came up behind him.

He spun around to face her. "I thought this was only supposed to take an hour. What's going on in there?"

Her expression softened and she waved him off with a hand. "You are thinking in terms of Earth procedures. Mathezar will complete the treatment today, so you had better get a move on with your studies, since you will need the information for tomorrow's duties." She paused a moment. "Are you following Tounga's schedule or just superimposing a cadet schedule to his?"

Tommy shifted his stance and furrowed his brows. "I have no idea what you are asking me." He tried to make sense of her question. He was not following the standard cadet schedule; he was following Tounga's shifts. What exactly did superimposing a cadet schedule mean?

She smiled. "Tomorrow, Dr. Tounga does a double shift. Normally, first year cadets adhere to the cadet schedule. Second year cadets follow day and evening shifts along with their mentors, but third year cadets match the shifts, including doubles, nights and overtime."

"But I'm only a first year cadet." He pulled his digipad from his pant pocket and went over his schedule. Only the medical rotation had been plotted out on his calendar.

"You forget that specific training also adapts to the potential of each cadet. You are on your own path of evolution." She pointed to the small room off of Tounga's office. "Settle yourself in there and get going on your studies."

Tommy nodded and headed off to the front of medical bay, to where Petra had pointed. Surveying the tiny space, he let out a sigh. There was no room for anything other than the glass desk with its two chairs. Settling himself in the chair facing out into medical bay, rather than into Tounga's office, would allow Tommy to keep an eye on the treatment chamber.

"Welcome, cadet," the cool voice of the CPU sounded in his head. The tabletop began to glow from within and a series of windows popped up side by side. Tommy looked them over. He had more anatomy and physiology to review, a session in microbiology and metabolic bio-chemistry that opened, and then there was the prep for his duties tomorrow.

As soon as Tommy had identified his windows, they shrank away and moved to the top left hand corner of the table, leaving the anatomy and physiology to expand to the size of the table. A 3-D image of the respiratory system lifted off the table and slowly rotated. "Identify the trachea and describe its function." The question was heard only in Tommy's head. He touched the electrode he wore behind his ear and sighed, he really hated that thing. *It connects the larynx with the bronchial parts of the lungs,* Tommy thought to the CPU, then reached out to identify the trachea.

"Identify and explain the function of," the CPU said in his head as the alveoli lit up.

When the table went black Tommy leaned back in his chair and stretched. He glanced toward the treatment room and wondered if they were still at it. "How long have I been studying?"

"Four hours, thirty-seven minutes," the disembodied voice answered.

Tommy let out a breath. *We were only supposed to do three*, he shot the CPU. He stepped out of the small cubby of a room and was surprised when he spotted Dr. Tounga talking with the chief medical officer. He was sure Petra had said Mathezar was the one seeing to Watoo's treatment.

Tounga smiled and waved Tommy over. "I would like you to share the different treatments you may know of when we cover related matter in your training." Somehow his smile seemed to widen. "I can't believe the change that has come over Watoo."

"And in such a short time," Mathezar added, nodding satisfactorily.

Tommy felt relief wash over him. "I will," he said to Tounga. "Can I see him?"

"That will have to wait for tomorrow," Dr. Tounga answered. "He's gone to his quarters to sleep. He said he had to verify the training schedules for tomorrow and needed a good night's sleep."

Tommy closed his eyes and offered thanks for his friend's recovery.

"You are dismissed for the evening," Tounga said. "Check your schedule tomorrow morning before showing up. Watoo has been known to make last minute changes."

Tommy nodded and headed back to his quarters. He barely had time to step into the room when it happened again, only this time he was back on Earth. – *Quietly looking around, Tommy made sure he was alone. He slowly rose to peer into the window and dropped out of sight just as fast. The back of a bald Binari head was there, right at the window. His heart pounded in his ears. He looked around. The trough…he had never had the chance to fix the loose board on the chicken coop. He silently made his way over to the feeder and lifted it out of the snow. Relieved that it wasn't frozen to the ground, he moved it out of the way and pried open the loose board so he could squeeze through. The chickens were in the dark and didn't react to his intrusion. He closed his eyes and tried to control his breathing. Edging his way to the barn entrance, he caught a glimpse of the doctor's limp body, lying on the floor behind the commander.*

Something touched Tommy's shoulder and he jumped. A startled cry erupted from his depths as he feared the worst.

Chapter 8

"Thomas! Look at me," his father said. He held Tommy by the shoulders. "Why are you on the floor, what's wrong?"

Tommy swallowed shakily, letting himself get his bearings. With his father's help he stood and shakily made his way to the couch where he settled down onto it. This was the first time he'd had a flash of the past, and to top it off, the first time he'd acted out the scene. He could just imagine this happening around others. "I think I'm losing my mind."

His father remained calm, kneeling before his son. "Do you remember what happened?" His eyes searched Tommy's.

Tommy shook his head. "I'm not sure." He shuddered, pulled his knees up to his chest and wrapped his arms around them. "It was three years ago, and I was sneaking back into the barn. I saw you hanging by the feet, unconscious, saw the Binari…"

"What were you doing on the floor?" His father rose slowly and sat on the living room table in front of Tommy, which was totally out of character for the commander.

"I didn't want to be seen."

"So it wasn't just a memory, you were reliving it." The commander passed a hand over his mouth. "Mathezar, to my quarters."

Tommy jumped to his feet. "Father, no, please. I don't want anyone to know." He clenched his fists then wrapped his arms around himself. He was cold.

"Sit down, Thomas." He remained calm, following Tommy with his eyes. "Please." His tone softened, and he surrounded his son with comforting energy.

Tommy swallowed nervously and nodded, before he dropped unceremoniously onto the couch. He propped his elbows on his knees and held his head in his hands. He didn't bother looking up when the door chime sounded.

The doctor entered alone, much to Tommy's relief. He didn't need Jayden around right now. When the doctor touched Tommy he jumped again. It was almost as though his senses were in overdrive. "Lay back," the doctor said.

Both men helped Tommy stretch out and he could feel the doctor place the crystal disks on his wrists and temples. His body immediately relaxed and he felt the tension slip away. "Don't make me sleep, please," Tommy asked, afraid of being sucked away into another vision. The last thing he wanted was to have an episode in front of them.

The doctor let out a sharp breath. "The activity in his cerebral cortex is off the charts."

"Poison?" his father asked, laying a hand on Tommy's shoulder.

"No, this is something different." The doctor poked and prodded Tommy for a few minutes, not saying a word. "Can I remove your chip?"

Tommy snorted despite himself. "Need you ask?" Sobering a little, he made a move to sit up but was held in place by strong hands as the doctor removed the interface chip.

"Just relax until we figure this out," his father said. He turned his attention to the doctor. "I found him reliving a scene from his past, acting out."

The doctor considered the information. "Dthau-Mahsz, open the link and see if you can review the events," the doctor instructed. Tommy felt him adjust the disks and he slipped into a very light sleep. "Let yourself go, Thomas. We're right here."

Tommy nodded sleepily. He felt his father's presence, and watched in a detached way as the events of the past few days replayed in his mind. The commander did a double-take when he came to the visions of the future and ended up replaying the events a few times over as both the flash and the actual event. A wave of reassurance flowed through the link and Tommy slipped off into sleep.

When Tommy opened his eyes, he was relieved to find himself still on the couch, though the fact that the doctor was still present wasn't promising. "Can I sit up?" he asked before moving.

Mathezar stood and came to his side. "No, hold still another few minutes." He reached for the crystals on Tommy's temples and removed them. The wave of nausea that followed made it difficult to resist the doctor's orders, and Tommy doubled over on to his side.

"Drink this," the commander said as he gently lifted Tommy's head. The effect of the bitter drink was like a jolt of electricity through his body. He gagged on the second sip and was pulled into a sitting position, fully alert now.

"How do you feel now?" Mathezar asked.

Wiping his mouth with the back of his hand he looked around for something to rid himself of the terrible taste. "Was that one of Two-Feather's recipes gone bad?"

The corner of his father's mouth lifted into a smile. He reached for a different glass and handed it to Tommy. "Drink this one." He watched as his son drank half the glass in one sip. "Now, how do you feel?"

"What happened? What did you find?" He swung his legs off the sofa and leaned forward.

The commander settled across from his son, leaving the doctor at Tommy's side. "Give me your wrists," Mathezar said. He removed the crystal disks from Tommy's wrists and focused on the digipad readout.

Tommy was relieved that the nausea didn't return. He closed his eyes and composed himself.

"Well?" the commander prompted. "Can it be because I showed him how to access his memories through the link?"

"It shouldn't have that kind of effect on him." The doctor grimaced as he pointed to his readout. He flipped the readout towards the commander. "According to his records, his cerebral cortex had shown heightened activity the first time he came

onboard, but this is the first time it has happened since his return."
He shifted his attention to Tommy. "As far as I can tell, there is
nothing wrong with you, Thomas."

"Well, not all crazy people are sick," Tommy said discouraged.

"You are not crazy, Thomas," his father reassured him.

The doctor raised an eyebrow. "You have an idea?"

He pressed his lips together. "He saw images of the future," the
commander said, "and when I found him, the past. His premonitive
images are surprisingly accurate." He passed his hand over his
mouth.

"But that doesn't tell us what it is," the doctor said.

"Are you sure?"

"Father, please," Tommy cut in. He didn't like being discussed
as though he wasn't present, especially when his mental health was
in question.

"Do you not understand? It could not be anything else..." The
commander looked from the doctor to his son. "The gift, or ability,
the legend foretold of."

A heavy silence filled the room. "It's more like a curse,"
Tommy muttered. "The visions seem to be coming closer and
closer together, and I can't do anything to stop them, let alone
control them. How am I going to function if I keep throwing
myself on the ground in the middle of my shift? Or worse
yet...what if I hurt someone?" He threw his head back on the
couch and placed his hand on his forehead.

"You must learn to control them," his father said optimistically.

"You may even succeed in calling upon them at will."

"No, wait." The doctor started checking feverishly for information on his digipad. "There. This shows a shift in your cerebral cortex activity, just before the episode." He tapped away at his pad enthusiastically. "We could monitor you over a period of a few days and compare the physiological readings taken before, during and after your episodes." He pressed his lips together in thought.

The commander nodded. "We might be able to identify a trigger or a warning sign that one is on the way." He tugged on his uniform top.

"Come see me in the morning," the doctor said. "I'll install the monitor then." He turned to the commander. "It might be best to lock your door and set an alarm in case he gets up during the night, just to be on the safe side."

Tommy sat up straight to stare at the doctor and made a face. "Not very reassuring, Doc." He turned to his father. "Would this have happened to me had I still been on Earth?"

His father nodded. "You cannot change who you are, Thomas, only accept it."

Tommy inhaled deeply and considered his father's words. He'd have been locked up or put on anti-psychotic drugs on Earth. Either that or he'd have his own psychic hotline. "Then I suppose I'll see you in the morning, doctor."

The doctor stood, followed by the commander. "Thank you again, Mathezar," the commander said.

Mathezar quickly packed up his stuff and exited with a nod of his head.

Tommy was wide awake now, and except for feeling a little stiff, he was ready to face another day. His father eyed him closely. "The effects of the tonic will wear off in a few minutes, so I would suggest you avoid making any plans." He sat back down, across from his son.

Tommy held his father's gaze. He wondered if his amethyst eyes were as amazing as his father's. "I remember now," Tommy said, sitting up. "You never went into any details, but you had said that every person with amethyst eyes had shown some sort of ability." He searched his father's face. "You can sense people. You know when someone comes around, and you even know who it is. Am I right?"

His father nodded slowly.

"Do you know what the others can do?" Tommy asked, bursting with curiosity.

"No, although the rumors of the gifts are widespread, no one has ever shared any information on their gift." He stood.

Tommy felt his energy start to falter. "I guess I had better get to bed before I end up spending the night on the couch." He stood and took a step towards his room, stopped and turned. "Do you have any other *gifts*, Father?"

A smile spread across his father's face, lighting his eyes with mischief. "Good night, Thomas."

It was happening again, only this time Tommy was in the middle of a dream and the images overlapped, causing some kind of sensory overload. Confused, he pushed up from his bed and tried to situate himself. Strong arms slammed him back down and a putrid smell filled his nostrils. Before he could gag or even cry out an alarm sounded, startling the smelly thing holding Tommy down. Taking advantage of the momentary lax, Tommy rolled onto his back and brought a knee up, connecting with his attacker who let out a satisfying grunt. Launching himself off the bed, he made a dash for the door, but someone or something slammed him face first into the wall. A sharp stab of pain to the back of his shoulder terrified him. *Help me!* He called out through the link. Searing pain ripped through his back as a metallic taste filled his mouth. He couldn't breathe. The lights came on just as his world went black.

The throbbing of Tommy's head hit home like an axe splitting wood. The slightest movement proved to be excruciating. Confused and weak, he lay there in the dark, letting his senses return. The hair at the back of his neck bristled. He wasn't alone.

His heart raced out of control and he gulped down some air. He felt the link flare out of fear, as he tried desperately to make contact with his father. No response, nothing other than a faint glimmer of his existence. Tommy struggled in vain, but he couldn't sit up. His hands had been tied behind his back. The sting of tears burned his eyes as he lay in a heap on a cold, hard floor. This wasn't a dream.

His heart rate took off again when he heard a shuffling sound. He strained unsuccessfully against the darkness to see, but couldn't make out anything. *Thomas!* His father reached out through the link and relief washed through him.

Where are you, Father? What happened? Where am I? Tommy blurted out. Something was off. *Are you OK?*

Do you still have your pocket knife in your jumpsuit? His father asked.

How did you know? He couldn't believe his father knew. Ever since he'd gotten lost on a strange planet, he'd vowed to never be without certain items.

Yes, or no?

Yes, he answered cautiously.

Slide over to me and place yourself so I can access your knife.

You're here? So much for being rescued by his father this time… A feeling of dread grew in the pit of his stomach.

Focus on the sound. Move closer as quietly as possible so as not to alert them that we have regained consciousness. A slight scraping sound came from behind Tommy. He rolled and shifted, clenching his teeth to not make a sound, no matter how much the maneuver hurt. He forced himself into a sitting position and scooted closer to his father. He listened carefully for the sound to come again. He inched his way over to what he hoped was his father.

Bumping up against his father's back he felt the ties that held his father's hands in place. *Turn so I can reach your knife.*

Tommy shifted, bringing his leg to his father's hands. He couldn't believe the people who attacked them hadn't taken it; at least he hoped they hadn't.

Bring your hands to me.

Tommy inched lower, until he touched his father's hands, and the knife. *Do you want me to do it, Father?*

Hold still, I do not want to hurt you.

Tommy felt the blade of the knife as his father attempted to slip it between his wrists to cut the ties. Footsteps outside the room made them stiffen, and Tommy's breath caught. His heart pounded wildly in his ears as his father worked the blade. He stifled a gasp as the blade cut into his wrist and he jerked away as the ties fell, freeing his hands. Clenching his teeth, he took the knife from his father and cut the ties as quickly and carefully as possible.

Muffled voices from outside the room grew louder. They were just outside the door.

Give me the knife and lie back down. Close your eyes and don't move.

The door slid open and the retched smell of Tommy's attacker wafted in. "They're still out," a gruff voice said with a laugh. "I hit them good and hard."

"Well I hope for your sake it wasn't too hard," a nasal voice said. "He wants the commander to watch him kill his son." The door slid shut, taking with it the light and last words of their abductors.

Tommy sat up, pure terror overpowering him. *Do not give in to your fear, Thomas.* The link expanded and Tommy felt his father's strength surround him.

Father, we don't know where we are or even how many of them there are. There's no one we can call for help... Tommy's thoughts died away. He didn't want to die. He didn't want his father to have to watch.

There are only three in proximity. I do not know who or even what they are. He paused. *You must use your gift. Focus and try to see something, anything.*

I will try Father, but I don't know how to make one happen. His father's energy grew stronger, bringing Tommy to the moments preceding his last premonition hoping to provoke another one. – *Tommy was in the arboretum, kneeling in the dirt as Fardoc circled him, taunted him. His face was swollen and bloodied, his uniform in tatters. Leering, Fardoc dragged a thorn covered branch across Tommy's back and laughed.*

Lifting his eyes, Tommy caught his father's tear stained face. His legs had been broken; his hands crushed, and now he sat, forced to watch as they tortured his son. "I only need your eyes," Fardoc said sadistically, "but I could not resist the urge to take them slowly. He opened his arms wide and spread his fingers as he threw his head back and filled his lungs. "This is so invigorating!" he cried

Tommy gagged as bile rose in his throat. What good was it to have such a gift if there was nothing he could do to prevent the outcome? His whole body trembled.

Do not give in to the vision, Thomas! We must use the knowledge to change the outcome.

But that's not possible! Everything I've seen so far has happened as I saw it play out in the flashes. He drew his knees up and leaned heavily on his father. He didn't want to die...not that way. He thought of Jayden, of the feelings that had been growing for her lately. He thought of how torn she'd be losing a close friend. He knew she'd not yet gotten over the loss of her mother...he should have suggested using the same treatment on Jayden that had worked on Watoo. Watoo...he'd never see his friend again. Tears streamed down his face.

Thomas! Now is not the time to give up. Get up. Let's position ourselves on each side of the door and try and take them by surprise.

Standing shakily, Tommy offered a hand to his father. He took it, much to Tommy's surprise. Slowly, with arms outstretched, they made their way to where the door had opened. His father leaned heavily on Tommy's shoulder. *What's wrong? What did they do to you?*

I'm fine. Take your position. Do you want your knife?

Tommy recoiled. *No, you keep it. I wouldn't be able to use it...*

Take your position, someone is coming.

Butterflies danced around in Tommy's stomach and his ears seemed to block. He felt reassurance flow from his father and he drew on the much needed energy. Leaning back against the cold wall, he tried to control his breathing. He had to fight for his life, for his father, for Jayden. He let his mind wander to the last time they'd talked, to reaching out and touching her cheek, to how soft her skin had seemed.

Focus, Thomas, here they come.

Tommy's legs felt like lead as he braced himself for their captor's entrance into the room. Mouth open, he tried to control his breathing, to regain some sense of calm. His father was obviously hurt and Tommy needed to be the strong one. Using the link he went back to his karate lessons, to the sparring, the competitions, and drew the strength he needed from the memory.

Alert now, he felt adrenaline rush through his veins and he clenched his jaw. The voices grew louder, and Tommy shifted instinctively into a fighting stance.

The door opened and the attackers entered without looking. They were too busy sneering and spewing obscenities to notice their captives were no longer on the floor where they'd left them. One step into the dimly lit room and they stopped dead in their tracks. That was the moment Tommy had been waiting for. He jumped into action, slamming a side kick into the closest captor's lower back, bringing him to his knees. Spinning around, Tommy's leg shot out and his heel connected with the side of the other's head, causing it to snap back and Tommy saw him drop to the ground

A burst of pain came through the link from his father. Tommy gasped as he turned to where his father had been standing. Something hit him hard between the shoulder blades, knocking the wind out of him. Tommy was sent sprawling across the floor. Strong arms lifted his upper body off the ground and he felt the sharp pain as a foot connected with his jaw. He was unceremoniously thrown face down and dragged from the room by the legs, still gasping for air as he tried to spit out the blood.

Dirt filled Tommy's mouth and nose as his captor dragged him across the ground, forcing him to struggle and squirm to keep his head up. Were they in the arboretum? His legs, now released, slammed heavily into the ground as the one who had been dragging him spun around and viciously kicked him in the ribs. Tommy curled up into a ball on his side, heaving from the pain. All he could see at this point were black spots forming and growing before his eyes. He choked on his blood and vomited as he desperately tried to catch his breath. Each attempt to breathe, to move, caused a blinding pain as his injured ribs dug into his side. He had failed. Well, at least he wouldn't be alive to relive the scene from his premonition. *I'm sorry Father,* Tommy sent through the link, *I love you. Goodbye, Jayden, I –*

"Everybody stay where you are!" a booming voice filled the room. Footsteps scurried all around as orders were called out and shots fired. Tommy felt himself slipping away. He reached out one last time to find his father and was relieved to sense a strong but unresponsive presence. He was probably unconscious, but that was OK, it was reassuring to know his father was safe now. It didn't matter what happened to him anymore, just so long as his father was ok. He could let go…his body hurt so much…he couldn't breathe…time to let go.

"Don't you dare leave me," Jayden was whispering in his ear. "You hold on, you hear me?" She was wiping the hair from his face while she held his hand. "Medical emergency!" She sounded frantic.

A burst of emotion came through the link, taking Tommy by surprise since it wasn't from his father. A jumbled mass of every emotion possible sparked and faded as quickly as it appeared. Jayden. It was Jayden.

Opening his eyes he knew he was still alive. The pain was too intense for him to be dead, but if something wasn't done to ease it soon he'd want to be dead. His heart rate became suddenly erratic, and his breathing labored as he slipped back into oblivion.

He awoke screaming, his arms flailing about as he fought off his attacker. "Stop! Thomas stop, you're OK," Petra's voice broke through his struggle. "You're safe now. It's over."

Within seconds, Tommy felt his father's presence through the link and a hand on his shoulder. Breathing heavily, he struggled to sit up and was surprised at how much his body hurt. "Easy," his father said soothingly. "Lay back and let Mathezar finish."

Tommy let himself fall back onto the warm glasslike exam table and felt it readjust to his body's contour. "How long have I been here?" Tommy's mouth was sore and swollen.

"Not long enough," Petra said. "Now lie back and wait for Mathezar to deal with you." She stepped out of the particle curtain, leaving Tommy alone with his father.

"How come you're up and about?" Tommy asked, immediately regretting the effort.

The link expanded between the two. "I'm fine, Thomas. Just a few bruises," he said softly. You took the brunt of the attack."

I'm sorry I failed you Father.

"You know how I feel about what you did to save me." There was an uncomfortable silence between the two, and then his father answered through the link. *I would like to discuss security and defense strategy with you. I find myself in unknown territory, for never before has there been an open assault on a crisis intervention ship. You seem to understand this somewhat more than I do.*

OK, Father, we will discuss it once I stop hurting.

"Mathezar!"

Tommy let a laugh slip and his damaged ribs immediately protested.

"Let that be a lesson to you," Mathezar said. He paused for a moment and looked down at Tommy, concern in his eyes. "The best thing would be to put you in stasis so we ca –"

Tommy grabbed the doctor's arm as his heart rate kicked up another notch. *Father please…*

Let him finish, Thomas, or I will have him put you under and treat you. I have the feeling he is trying to accommodate your fear of our procedures.

The doctor placed the crystal disks on his forehead and wrists and Tommy began to relax. "What I am proposing is this," Mathezar said calmly. "I can put you in stasis long enough to set everything and after a few hours I will allow you to return to your quarters under strict bed rest. Or, I can do all my procedures with you conscious, but it will take longer and I will not release you for at least forty-eight hours.

It hurts too much, Father, even with the disks...just make it stop.

When Tommy opened his eyes he was surprised not only to find himself in his own bed, but to have Jayden at his side. When their eyes met she smiled down at him with a tenderness he had never before seen from her. He never would have imagined her capable of such a look. For a moment they held each other's gaze and he was shocked when she reached out to brush the hair from his forehead. Reaching for a glass she offered him a straw to sip the farou tonic.

Laying the glass aside she reached for a damp cloth and sponged his face with care causing a spark to ignite inside of him. Sliding the sheets down to expose his chest she continued her care, sponging his neck and shoulders. When she went to move lower he caught her hand and shook his head 'no'.

The more his mind cleared, the more he became aware of just

how sore he was. Pain seared through him.

Almost as though she was reading his thoughts, she took his wrist and turned it over with skilled precision to adjust the dosage on the medipad. Relief washed through him and he took his first deep breath since the incident.

"What are you doing here?" he asked, his jaw stiff and sore.

"Hmm, you'd think it would be obvious." She studied the readout on her med scanner. "OK, you should be good for now. Would you like me to help you to the bathroom?"

Father!

Tommy's bedroom door opened and the commander stepped in. "Leave us," he said to Jayden.

"Sir, but I was –"

He turned to face her, and Tommy watched as he held her gaze, an eyebrow lifting slowly, daring her to protest. "You may return to your duties. I will tend to his needs for now."

With a muffled sound of protest she left the room, leaving father and son alone.

"We need to talk," his father said in a tone that left Tommy confused.

"Did I do anything wrong?" He shifted in his bed uncomfortably.

"No, but we need to discuss how or rather why we were rescued." His father maintained his initial position by the door. "I will help you to the shower and will prepare some food while you wash. We will discuss it then."

Tommy nodded, more confused than ever. He lifted his covers to sit up and realized he was naked. Knowing Jayden had been sitting at his side while he lay there without any clothes made him uncomfortable, and he felt his face flush. His father helped him slip into a bath robe and steadied him as he got shakily to his feet.

Clean and well fed, Tommy relaxed on the couch across from his father. "You said you wanted to discuss how or why we were rescued. Were we not meant to be saved?" Tommy had thought about his father's comment while showering but it didn't make any sense.

"What was the last thing you remembered before the rescue?" His father's eyes held his gaze in a sharp, analytical way.

Tommy pressed his lips together and searched his memory. "About the attack?"

The commander shook his head slowly. "Your thoughts. What were you thinking?"

Tommy felt his face heat as he remembered. He swallowed and took a deep breath. "I said goodbye to you, that I loved you…"

His father nodded and gave him a half smile. "Was there anything else…anyone else?"

"Jayden," Tommy whispered. He cleared his throat. "Why?"

His father let out a breath and sat across from Tommy. "Jayden stormed the arboretum with a security detail. I have yet to know what she told them to get them to move so quickly." He passed a hand across his mouth. "What do you remember of our bonding or mating rituals?"

"What are you talking about?" They must have hit his father on the head harder than the doctors had noticed.

An eyebrow shot up as the commander eyed his son. "I assure you that my 'head' is fine."

"I'm sorry Father, but I fail to understand what you want from me." Tommy knew a mate was for life and that they shared a special bond…but what did that have to do with him?

"Do you love her?" His question held no emotion, no hint of approval or other.

Tommy stood and began to pace nervously. "I don't know…"

"But you do have feelings for her." It wasn't a question. "Please, sit, or the doctor will be dragging you back to medical bay." His gaze was steady as he waited for an answer.

He realized there was no sense in trying to deny his feelings because he'd probably broadcast them through the link at one time or another. "Yes, and I'm not quite sure what to do about that."

His father chuckled softly. "Some things are out of our control." A smile drifted from his lips.

"You're referring to Mom, aren't you?" He drew in a long breath. "What if Jayden doesn't feel the same way?" He was surprised at how easy it was to talk about this with his father, but then the link left little hidden.

"Thomas, she heard you, your plea. She felt your distress." He sobered. "You are both very young for this form of attachment to manifest itself, and the extent of your connection should only become that intense after bonding." His gaze drifted away, lost in thought.

"We didn't bond." He wasn't sure what to make of his father's reaction. It's not like they'd been caught 'together'.

His father coughed, obviously catching the last of Tommy's thoughts. He composed himself and straightened. "You are not thinking as a strategist."

Tommy did a double take. "You mean as someone they could hold against me." He rested his forehead in his hand. "Father I don't know what to do." He made a move to get up but his father held out a hand.

"Remain sitting and take a deep breath," his father ordered. "The doctor is monitoring your vitals and if you become too agitated he'll know. If you wish to remain here, then you will have to stay calm." He watched as Tommy took a moment to settle. "Good, now you may continue."

Furrowing his brows, Tommy shook his head in discouragement. "I have been wrestling with so many things lately, and having to add the extra responsibility of Jayden's safety…" He let out a breath.

"You are referring to whether your place is here or back on Earth?" The commander held his son's gaze, while his own expression gave nothing away.

Tommy nodded without answering. "I wasn't sure where I should be, but I believed that I could be of more use to my planet from here." He shifted in place. "I also believed that if anything happened to either of us, then the other would be able to help, but I never thought we'd be taken at the same time." He clenched his fists and brought them to his head. "And now there's Jayden..."

His father nodded gravely. "All things to take into consideration."

The hair on Tommy's arms prickled as he remembered the attack. "Where is Fardoc? How did they even get onboard the ship?" He shuddered. "How is it possible for someone to just come aboard?"

Passing a hand over his mouth, the commander exhaled sharply. "Since the beginning of our existence as the guardians of our sister colonies, we have been treated with respect. Even in the odd case when two colonies were torn by conflict, no one targeted us."

"Does this ship even have any weapons?"

"Yes. We have a security detachment as well as a full array of armament, though I do not believe there has been a recorded case of the ship having to fight, and we have never been at war, not even amongst ourselves."

The last statement settled on Tommy. He could not imagine growing up in such a utopian-type society. "Is any of this my fault?"

He shook his head. "No, and I don't want you to ever think that," he said reassuringly.

"And Fardoc?"

"He is being held separate from those he enlisted on his quest." His tone became sharp, his eyes cold. Tommy felt a flash of emotion from his father that unsettled him. To say that he was angry with Fardoc was an understatement, but somehow Tommy got the impression his father was in unchartered waters where these emotions were concerned.

"What does 'held separate' mean exactly? Don't tell me you don't have a brig."

The expression on his father's face was unreadable. "He has been confined to his quarters."

"His quarters? The same ones he'd occupied before? Was the dungeon full?" Tommy's mind ran through all sorts of scenarios. He could see the evil Fardoc planning for such an event, hiding material to plan an escape or worse, an attack. "Why don't you have a jail, holding cell, dog carrier...anything to keep him locked up!"

"There is a security detail at his door, he cannot go anywhere." A strange bell chimed and the commander rose in one fluid movement and headed for the replicator. He returned a moment later with two glasses. "Here, we have been instructed to consume this." He handed one to Tommy.

Making a face, and afraid to smell it, Tommy held the glass at arm's length. He watched his father closely for any sign of revulsion as he drank his.

Setting his glass down, the commander raised an eyebrow. "It is safe."

Cautiously, Tommy brought the glass to his lips, careful not to smell it. He drank half the glass in one large gulp, surprised when he realized that the dark brown liquid was actually pleasant tasting.

He set the glass down.

"You have to finish it all, and if you want the taste to last, don't wait." His father advised.

Frowning, and without wasting time, Tommy downed the second half in a second gulp. "Ugh! What did he put in there, sewer water?"

"You never know."

Tommy's head snapped up to get a look at his father. He pushed the glass across the table, but his father removed it and returned the two to the replicator. "Before the smell overtakes our quarters."

"I don't think Two-Feathers has ever made anything that smelly or foul tasting before," Tommy said, his upper lip curling from the aftertaste.

"Hmm, well you can thank your shaman for it nonetheless. It would seem that the good doctor has been experimenting on his own."

"So that's why he let me out of medical bay, so this stuff wouldn't stink up the place?" He shifted again, unable to find a comfortable position. "I thought you were in bad shape. How come you look normal?"

"I had lost consciousness, so they did not attack me as they did you," his father said grimly.

"Well, if I'm OK and you're OK, then what's the problem?" Tommy asked.

"I have some decisions to make. Some changes to implement."

He watched his father closely and saw the concern in his eyes, the flash of distaste. "You don't like the idea of taking a formal defensive stance, even if it's only to be ready to defend rather than attack."

His father shook his head. "It goes against everything we have ever stood for. We have never had to fight for or against anything or anyone." He let out a sigh laden with disgust. "I don't even know where to start."

"I can help, Father. We can at least be ready to defend ourselves, and take some simple precautions." He pulled himself up a little straighter. "I still can't understand how people can just come aboard without permission. It's not safe and doesn't make sense."

"Could you prepare a plan of action, along with some suggestions that we could go over later?" He paused to study Tommy. "You look as though you are very uncomfortable. Maybe you should get some more sleep and we will continue this tomorrow."

As if on cue, Tommy's achiness abated and he was able to think clearly. Maybe the doctor's concoction wasn't so bad after all. His mind whipped back to Fardoc and the holding arrangements. "Did you search his quarters before he was sent there? How do you know he didn't stock up on stuff so he could escape if ever he was punished again?"

Color drained from his father's face. "When I had checked in with security earlier, I did not have them check inside..."

The door to their quarters opened and a frantic Mathezar burst into the room. "I can't find Jayden anywhere, and I cannot connect with her through the link."

"Security, locate Fardoc!" the commander shouted out. "Confirm with visual that all detainees are present and accounted for."

"Doctor, check how many people are onboard through your database." At the doctor's raised eyebrow, Tommy insisted. "Just do it, please." He remembered the doctor having more information regarding 'all souls onboard' versus the commander's personnel list. "And cross-reference with my father's info."

An overwhelming burst of emotion grabbed Tommy and knocked the breath out of him. He shut his eyes, fighting the wave of sickening fear. He dropped to his knees, gasping. "He's got her…"

–Fardoc circled Jayden as he taunted her at the base of the waterfall. Somehow he knew Jayden couldn't swim very well. He stood on a ledge above the water and pushed her into the deep basin, leering as she splashed about frantically, struggling to keep her head above water. Overshadowing her, he lifted his foot above her head and pushed her under again.

"Commander, Fardoc is no longer in his quarters but the other three are accounted for." The voice of a security officer boomed through the communication system, pulling Tommy from his vision.

"Maintain visual contact with each one, and do not leave your post," the commander ordered.

"They're in the arboretum," Tommy blurted out when he recognized the body of water he'd designed.

"Security! I want the ship on silent, critical alert. Have all personnel clear the corridors. Send a security team to the arboretum." The commander paused a moment. "No one enters until I arrive."

None of this would have happened had I not come onboard, Tommy thought bitterly. He hurried ahead of the two others, hoping to get another flash so he could come up with a plan of action. He prayed Jayden hadn't been thrown into the water yet.

Assembling outside the arboretum, Tommy stopped his father from entering. "Couldn't we just transport in, or transport Jayden out of there?"

"He's blocking her signal," Mathezar said.

Tommy pressed his lips together, thinking hard. "I saw Jayden in the pool at the waterfall." He looked at his father. "Could you locate them? You have the —"

His father held up a hand to silence him and closed his eyes. Tommy opened the link and offered to share the vision with his father, hoping it would help.

After what seemed like the longest pause ever, the commander opened his eyes and gave instructions to his security guards in a low voice. The dozen men nodded in silence before slipping into the arboretum.

The blonde security guard that remained behind took position next to the doctor.

"Stay here, Doctor, this won't take long." Through the link all he said to Tommy was, *follow.*

The doctor neither protested nor attempted to come along, and this disturbed Tommy. He forced his attention back to the situation as he moved to follow his father into the arboretum. There was no way he was going to stay behind.

Another wave of fear hit Tommy, and he grabbed hold of the link with his mind to reach out and comfort Jayden. He focused all of his attention on the link, not noticing his father had come to a stop until he slammed into him.

Stifling a cry, he righted himself and took a look at the reason they were no longer moving. An unfamiliar force field of sorts glowed softly just inside the door. Now what were they to do?

Shifting his weight nervously, Tommy watched as his father removed a wall panel and punched in a set of commands. The force field shifted, dimmed and came back as strong as before.

The commander drew in a breath and tried another combination. The panel sparked wildly before it went dark, but the force field remained unaffected.

Tommy let out a grunt of frustration just as the light shifted and the barrier faded. *Follow,* came again through the link.

In silence, the two men made their way cautiously through the dense tropical section of the arboretum. Mindful of where he stepped, Tommy did a double-take when he saw that his father moved about with his eyes closed. The sound of water flowing grew as they moved deeper into the arboretum, and Tommy strained to hear what was going on.

Jayden's fear rose again and Tommy opened his side of the link to her, opened his heart and memories. His breath caught when he realized he could feel her heart beat, and sense what was in the deepest part of her soul. He had to get to her.

Cries and the sound of splashing caught his attention. No! Fardoc was going to throw her in. *Remember what Peter taught you*, he called out to her through the link.

They rounded the bend in time to see Jayden go under, and Fardoc delight in her distress. Outraged, Tommy bent down to scoop up a fist sized rock. Taking a stance, he shifted the rock in his grip, squeezed it tight before he threw it like a fast ball. It hit Fardoc behind the ear with a satisfying thud, and the tormentor dropped to one knee. Covering the terrain in a few large strides, Tommy dove into the pond, fully dressed, and hurried to push Jayden back up to the surface.

"Don't fight me," he said in a firm voice as he shifted her onto her back and supported her with an arm. He tried to make his way back to the edge of the basin, only to meet with resistance.

"I'm stuck, you won't be able to pull me out," she sputtered, coughing up water. She started to panic.

Mind racing, he patted down the length of her body and felt the sharp jab from the thorny vines that held her in place. Treading water, he reached for his pocket knife and started cutting away the vines, while struggling to support them both. "Work with me Jayden, trust me." They sank down enough to swallow a mouthful of water then bobbed back up. "Just lie back, don't fight me." Tommy, weighed down by his wet clothing and a frantic Jayden, slipped under again as she thrashed about. Forcing his head above water, he tightened his grip on Jayden. "Calm down or we'll both drown!" His lungs burned from the water he choked up.

Jayden's body shuddered under his hold, sparking a protective reflex within Tommy. "Shhh, you're safe now," he said as he bought her even closer to him. "Everything will be all right." Jayden fell silent as the last of the vine fell away, and Tommy kicked for shore where his father waited with a security detachment.

Jayden was lifted from Tommy's arms and her father pulled her into a tight hug. Tommy paused to catch his breath on the shoreline, waving his father's hand off. After a few minutes, he pulled himself to his feet, catching Jayden's eye. A spark of emotion, of electricity, passed between them. The corner of his mouth lifted as she dropped her gaze, but the feeling remained.

Fardoc, face down in the dirt, moved lethargically as security lifted him to his feet, and forcedly carted him off. His face was bloodied and he avoided making eye-contact with anyone. The fight seemed to have left Fardoc, but Tommy didn't trust the likes of him. Dragging his gaze from the man that filled Tommy with more anger than he'd ever felt, Tommy turned toward his father. Shocked to see the commander covered in dirt and sweat, he searched for signs of injury.

The commander smiled, shaking his head. "I am fine. I will

follow security and deal with Fardoc."

Tommy had been pacing his quarters for over an hour and by now he'd used up all of his patience. He would have preferred to have stayed with Jayden, but she'd gone off with her father, and Tommy wasn't about to interrupt them -especially if they could finally reconnect. Not following her had been really difficult; however, being alone with no news from anyone was worse.

"Where is my father?" Tommy barked out at the CPU.

"The commander's location has not yet changed. You had asked to be informed when there would be a change." The monotone male voice sounded impatient.

"Just tell me when he's done." Tommy walked full circle around the room again, then headed right out the door to security with a determined gate. He had a rotation coming up here too, and now seemed like a good time to test the waters.

The security chief escorted Tommy to where his father sat, outside a holding cell, questioning Fardoc. Two guards flanked the prisoner as he answered. "No, I am not working with the Binari!" he scoffed. "They are primitive imbeciles, believing in superstitions and folktales." He pointed to the pair of amethyst crystals on the table in front of the commander. "They held enough crystals to generate power beyond what anyone had ever seen before, and they made a necklace out of them!" His voice took on its annoying whine, and the security guard to his left motioned for him to calm down.

"Then why did you get involved in this?" Tommy looked over the repulsive man.

Fire flared in Fardoc's eyes, and the veins in his neck bulged as two tiny lights from an electrode placed there lit up. "Power...it's all about power." An air of disgust colored his features as he looked down on Tommy. "Your people could have had dominion over so many planets, and yet you never sought to take control."

"I've heard enough," the commander said to the chief of security. "Escort him to a shuttle, get him off my ship."

Tommy looked up to see Kurok in the far corner of the room, exchanging glances with the chief. "Shall I accompany him, Commander?"

"No, I have already given my orders to the chief." He rose, tugged on his uniform top and nodded for Tommy to follow him out.

"Are you sending him back for more rehabilitation?" Tommy asked his father as they made their way back to their quarters.

"No, we have already seen that avenue fail." He went silent a moment. "He is on his way to Trygus III."

"To train to be a better warrior?" Tommy didn't know what to think.

"No, he was captured in a failed attempt. They will handle him in a most unpleasant way, and I doubt he will ever try again...if he survives." He stepped aside to let Tommy enter their quarters. The pair moved silently and settled across from one another in the common area.

Tommy didn't care to know what waited for Fardoc. "Can you be certain he won't try again?"

The commander nodded. "The doctor implanted a chip used long ago by those who oversaw our security. It obliges the bearer to tell the truth and act in a more appropriate manner. It broadcasts their position, eliminating the possibility of any form of a sneak attack. Not something any criminal wants in their midst." He pressed his lips together in thought.

"What now?" Tommy asked.

The commander leaned forward, his eyes staring into Tommy's. "We will revise our security proceedings. You will share your knowledge."

Tommy nodded. "It doesn't hurt to be cautious, and it doesn't make you a bad person to be prepared. It's not as though you were being more aggressive, just more aware, more prepared." He paused, trying to see the change from his father's point of view. "I can't imagine it being worse than having a verndari."

The commander visibly relaxed. "I guess not." He held Tommy's gaze. "Thank you. Now, let's get started."

Later that evening, Tommy and Jayden sat alone on the observation deck staring out into space, waiting for Earth to come into view. The arboretum had always been their preferred spot, but after what they'd just been through, they had decided to avoid it.

She leaned on his shoulder as they stared out at the stars in silence, and Tommy couldn't help but enjoy the feeling of having her close.

She tilted her head upward and watched him. "Are you still trying to figure out whether you should stay or not?" Leave it to Jayden to cut to the chase.

He let out a bitter laugh. "If only it was that easy." He dropped his eyes to meet hers, and brushed a lock of hair from her forehead.

She pushed away from him and sat up to face him. "Isn't it?"

He searched her face to see if she was joking. "Seriously? Would you mind telling me how you see it?"

She drew her knees up to her chest, wrapped her arms around them and then shrugged. "I get the wanting to go back. There's not one day that goes by where I wouldn't want to stop my mom from going down on that planet and never coming back. I keep thinking of what my life was like and how it should have been, but I've come to realize that every moment spent in the past is a moment wasted in the present..." her voice trailed off. She dropped her eyes and looked away from Tommy's as they began to fill with tears.

She drew in a steadying breath and raised her head as she squared her shoulders. "Change sucks." She shot him a glance and pressed her lips together, having used Jason's favorite expression to stress her point. "Once again, we find ourselves stuck in the middle of change. Not sure of where we're going, and no longer willing to remain where we are." She laid a hand on his knee.

He covered her hand with his own and gave it a light squeeze. "I agree, but there is so much more at stake here. There are so many things up in the air, I don't know what to do and I can't help but think if I hadn't come into this world, things wouldn't be so messed up."

She tilted her head and grimaced. "You are going to have to explain that to me," she said bluntly.

He shifted uncomfortably and let out a forced breath. "Come on Jayden. If it hadn't been for me, none of this stuff with the Binari would have happened. Fardoc would be somewhere terrorizing cats instead of people, and my father would not have to devise a security plan or put up with attacks and outbreaks of violence." His voice trembled with disgust.

"And how exactly is any of that your fault?" she asked softly.

"The Binari –"

She held up a hand to stop him. "They were after your father."

He shook his head. "Creighton and his father were involved."

"Yes, and they had been planning to take your father. You were a bonus." Her tone was blunt. "Whether you had come here or not, an attempt would have been made. Your father is probably alive because you are here."

He looked off into space, hoping Earth would soon come into view. He paused a moment to think, avoiding her gaze. "My father said that your people have never had to fight for anything or anyone, nor did you have to defend yourselves," he tried again.

Jayden scoffed. "Because the Forefathers oversaw our safety for the longest time."

Tommy grabbed her wrist. "I was told they left this galaxy something like a thousand years ago." He didn't believe her.

She nodded. "Yes, but they had left behind a kind of patrol or safety unit. The last of them died out," she paused and pressed her lips together. "I'd say twenty years ago or so."

Tommy scrunched his eyebrows. "Yet no one felt like taking their place?"

She closed her eyes and shook her head. "That's not the way it's done around here, Earth boy." A delicate hand flew to cover her mouth as she tried unsuccessfully to stifle a laugh.

He made a move for her but she stopped him by pointing to the observation window. He shot a glance over his shoulder and watched as Earth grew before his eyes. There were no words to describe the feeling of awe as his home appeared and filled the window. He felt Jayden's hand as it came to rest on his forearm and he slid an arm around her waist, pulling her close to his side.

"Whatever happens to your planet will not be your fault, and you alone would not be able to prevent it." She leaned in to him. "At least you'll be able to help if the need for an intervention does happen."

"I feel like I'm jumping ship while everyone else has to go down with it." He kept his eyes riveted to the window as the Phoenix settled into orbit around Earth. He wondered briefly how come the ship could settle into an orbit without being detected, but he figured he'd know soon enough.

The view was almost mesmerizing and Tommy found it hard not to stare at the swirls of clouds that covered the oceans and continents. He stole a glance in Jayden's direction, wondering why she'd gone silent but it appeared as though she too, had been caught under the spell of Earth's beauty. "It is one of the more beautiful planets in our galaxy," Jayden said.

"If ever I decide to stay on Earth, would you stay with me?" He stiffened when he realized he'd spoken the words out loud.

She pushed back and searched his eyes. "What exactly do you think you can do from home that would save your planet?"

He let out a long breath. "I don't know, Jayden, but after some of the devastation I've seen since I've come on board, I'd hate for it to happen to my planet." He pulled her back to him.

"She's survived in the past," she said absently.

Tommy froze at her words, needing a minute to let them sink in, before pushing her back at arm's length. He frowned, anger building inside. "Explain that. Tell me what you mean by that."

Jayden frowned, looking confused by his reaction. "Do you not know your own history?"

He shook his head. "Explain."

"Your planet has had the most interventions yet." She bent to retrieve her digipad from her pant pocket and tapped away at it. "Here's a list of civilizations that have had to have been relocated over time; the Olmec, the Nabateans, the Aksumite Empire, the Mycenaeans, the Clovis, the Minoans, the Anasazi, the Indus Valley Civilization, the Roanoke Colony, Lemuria, the Mayans,

Troy, Angkor…" She read off the list without pausing.

He didn't recognize more than a few of the names. "Are you sure? I mean I've heard of some, but where'd they go off to?" He tried to understand but it didn't make sense. There were still humans on Earth, so did that mean they'd been relocated from elsewhere as well?

"We'll go over the history lesson later," she said tugging on his arm. "I want to go back to the farm for a while. We might get to spend a few hours with your friends before the ship has to leave."

He held his ground. "I want your opinion on something." He waited for her to turn and face him.

"Which is?"

"What would you say if I told you I wanted to let my friends know the truth…?" He didn't finish his sentence.

Her face hardened. "The truth about what? Your planet? Your alien father? The fact that you live in space, on a ship?"

"Yes," he answered, his voice barely a whisper.

"Honestly, I think you should talk to your father about something like that." She shook her head in disbelief. "You might not get the reaction you expect."

Sitting by the lake, Tommy watched his friends as they dove into the water, off the long wooden pier, coaxing Jayden to follow suit. His father, Two-Feathers, the doctor and Grey Wolf, were all busy at the barbecue, an image that made Tommy laugh. The immediate critical situation had passed, Earth and her people would continue on, at least for now.

Something had shifted inside Tommy and he no longer felt like a child or a teen. Talking with Two-Feathers last night, he'd decided to ride the wave of change, and finally be honest with himself, his father and Jayden. His way of seeing things wasn't the same anymore; things were starting to make sense again. Tonight, he would tell his father that he will willingly take his place at his father's side, embrace his place in their society, and open both his arms and heart to Jayden. Well, OK, the last part he'd keep for just himself and Jayden, for the time being.

"You gonna sit out there all afternoon?" Peter called out to Tommy.

"Lunch is almost ready!" Mike's mom shouted to the group. Turning back to Tommy she added, "But you've got time for a swim."

Tommy grinned, pulled his jersey off with one arm and tossed it on the back of a chair as he made his way along the wooden planks to his friends in the water. He had planned on running and throwing himself in, making as big a splash as he could, but instead he paused, taking in the beauty that surrounded him. Everything was perfect, from the golden sunlight that sparkled and danced on the clear blue surface of the water, to the majestic Rockies that stood tall over them. He drew in a deep breath, filling his lungs, his soul, with pure mountain air. This, he would miss while onboard, but as Jayden had pointed out, now that they were considered to be adults, they would be able to return on their own every year.

Giggling from Jayden pulled him out of his thoughts, but not fast enough for him to catch on. Will plowed into him, sending him flying off the end of the pier and into the cool water of the lake. He felt the bubbles rise past his body as he let himself be brought up to the surface on his own. He caught Jayden's eye, and smiled. Tiny droplets of water clung to her eyelashes and her cheeks were rosy in the sunlight. He wanted to kiss her, but maybe now wasn't the right time. His smile broadened as she continued to stare into his eyes. He liked that.

"Thomas?" His father's voice pulled him from the memories of the day. Tommy looked up and registered his father's presence, then slowly, fluidly, stood from his perch in their porthole window. Earth had disappeared from view some time ago, but Tommy had let himself relive the memories through the link, as his father had shown him. "You said you had wanted to tell me something," his father continued.

Tommy pressed his lips together and nodded before making his way to the common area. Settling down onto the sofa, he gestured for his father to follow suit and suppressed a smile as he watched his dad tug characteristically on his uniform top. He tilted his head as he caught sight of the amused quirk to his father's mouth. "What's so funny, Father?"

Allowing the quirk to spread into a smile his father's amethyst eyes met and held Tommy's. "I believe this is the first time I sense that you are truly at peace with yourself, with your situation, and your choices."

Tommy nodded, breathing a sigh of relief. "I don't know why we bother to talk," he said. "You always know what's going on, even when I don't."

"It was a privilege to have had such an intense bond with you, my son." A look of sadness crossed his face and disappeared. "My assessment came from your body language, not the link. Your growing bond to Jayden will take up more room, and our contact will remain as more of a feeling, a discrete connection, without being invasive."

Well that was a relief, especially since Tommy had always had a tendency to broadcast everything to his father. He didn't feel like sharing anything that had to do with Jayden with anyone else.

The last of his worries dropped away. Earth was on an even tighter surveillance, so if things didn't level off, the Phoenix would be quick to intervene. Tommy had begun scouting for suitable planets, in the event of an evacuation, and the choice would be a personal one for him. That left his training, which he'd decided to embrace fully, and Jayden…whom he would embrace later on that evening.

About the author

All her life, Debbie has spun stories in her mind, watching characters come to life, seemingly by themselves. After working as a nurse, teacher, martial arts instructor, artist, and CIC officer in the Canadian military, (not to mention her many hobbies from woodworking to auto mechanics and holistic medicine), her life reads like a story itself. And yet, her favorite thing is still a cozy fire, a good book, and country living with her husband JP and her youngest of five children. After graduating from the Institute of Children's Literature's advanced writing course, she is finally devoting herself to writing these stories down, taking us all on a ride we won't quickly forget.

WEBSITE *http://bit.ly/18uGP3m*
BLOG *http://bit.ly/18NfYFB*
TWITTER *http://bit.ly/19aoqd3*
FACEBOOK *http://on.fb.me/IKQkoj*

www.ingramcontent.com/pod-product-compliance
Lightning Source LLC
Chambersburg PA
CBHW051434170626
46809CB00006B/2462